THE REMAINS OF CIVILISATION

ISBN 978-0-6480794-9-1

First Edition:
December 2018

THE
REMAINS
OF
CIVILISATION

YICHENG LIU

00

SO, I HAD A BRAVE AND VALIANT STARING CONTEST

with the business end of a gun. I happened to know for certain that the aforementioned gun had enough bullets inside it to not only kill me, but to miss a few times whilst doing so. I . . . didn't have a lot of faith in the shooter's shooting skills.

A few weeks prior, I had questioned exactly what I had done to deserve this. If there's an all-knowing God out there, it would stand to reason that I had pissed him off at some point in my life, or else *none* of this would've happened. If I were to ever make a list of my biggest crimes against humanity, it would begin with not brushing my teeth when I was eight and end with the stupid decision of reading the entire *Twilight* saga just to find out whether it was good or not (hint: it's a decision that I regret to this day).

At that point in time, I hoped desperately for a different ending to be in store for me instead of the usual "shot in the head and die" gimmick. Knowing what I know now . . . I still wouldn't bet on it. I comforted myself with the knowledge that, at the very least, I wasn't stupid enough to flail my arms around, screaming and wetting my pants at the same time. I kind of imagined that I would die with some dignity and have at least my best friend looking at me from the other side of a sterile white hospital room while a doctor mutters "It's going be okay" reassuringly to my imaginary family members whilst knowing full well it isn't. I wanna die old and satisfied in front of an annoyingly large group of people who are all weeping and just being miserable in general, bonus points if there's a young woman sharing a striking resemblance to me shaking me and yelling "Daddy, you'll make it! Please don't die on us! Everyone here will be absolutely miserable without your positive light within our existence." Ha, wouldn't that be great?

Heck, at least that way I could've made it my last request to ask the hospital to play annoying songs over the hospital's announcement speakers. That would've been the perfect ending to my life: dying as an old rich dude in front of loving family members and friends who gave a shit about me. Fuck you, I like that dream. It's not funny, stop laughing . . .

This, well, not so much. I was about to die unceremoniously from a bullet to the head, with my best friend gagged and hog-tied no more than five metres away from me. My eyes flickered to the woman behind him as well, lying on the ground, quite dead. It's not that it doesn't look cool or anything; in fact, I'm sure it would look great if this was a scene from a movie . . . but we happened to be on the top of a building. *In real life*. And I happened to be standing on the edge of said tall building with a gun pointed to my head—as I mentioned. The fact is, in the next minute or so, a nice bullet will probably decide to lodge itself into the space between my eyeballs. It won't matter if I somehow survive the shot; I will still become a nice splatter of meat and blood on the pavement below to presumably become trampled over by at least a few cars and at least one drunk truck driver spewing racist slurs for no reason at all. All that before anyone become aware of what I've become. It's not exactly how I expected my life to end. Nor is it the way I want it to end. ("By the way, is this, um, off the record?")

Anyways, look, I try to be a reasonable guy most of the time. I help out at the local food kitchens in December and send my relatives non-shitty gifts for Christmas. Heck, I even work out and go to gyms every now and then, so I don't really understand how I managed to lodge myself neck-deep in this mess. Honest. Just a normal, boring guy who does some mundane stuff. In fact, you'd be hard-pressed to find a logical sequence of events that could explain why I came to be standing on the ledge of a very tall building in the middle of nowhere at rush hour with no sign of police or any form of law enforcement within a two-kilometre radius. A random passer-by on the street would never see the gun pointed at my head or the man holding said gun from the haphazardly designed streets even if they had looked up.

And hence, I wanted to get the hell away from the gun barrel. Failing that, I had imagined at that point in time, the second-best-case-scenario would be for the wind to stop blowing into my face as I have really sensitive skin. There's a reason for the copious amount of pre-shave oil and vodka in the medicine cabinet.

"I want you to understand that you aren't supposed to be here," the man says as he theatrically waved his free hand about. "You really would never be here if it wasn't because of your curiosity. There isn't going to be a single thing that can save you from getting shot in the head." The man said as he casually waved his free hand about when he had realised that there wasn't an abundance of actions that could make him look more threatening, though I would've preferred it if he could wave that gun around a bit more, preferably away from my head.

Was it worth hoping for a miracle? Probably not. I had been starting to suspect it was the person upstairs that put me here in the first place.

Man, I was certain of my impending doom. The end of the line. Death would've come in a matter of moments if I fail to keep the guy monologuing. I had watched a lot of spy movies in my days, and I know that James Bond routinely hear more confessed sins against humanity than the average priest. Does that work in real life? I could give you two answers, and neither of which is a short yes. I wouldn't really say much came from it. As much as I would like to belittle the intelligence of someone who points a gun with the skill and accuracy of a drunken honey badger, the chances of him missing third and fourth and fifth shots are low.

As the wind blew a random paper bag into my face (it was *really* windy), I can't help but internally complain to myself about littering as I watched my life flash before my eyes. It's funny how you kind of get used to the fact that you're about to die when you had already been staring at the gun barrel for the better part of ten minutes. "*I should do this more often, preferably whilst listening to smooth Jazz and sipping an espresso martini,*" I thought, "*like the pathetic shitty off-brand James Bond-wannabe that I am.*"

As the man suddenly realised that I haven't exactly been paying attention to what he was saying for the last ten minutes, he mades a sound like the low guttural growl of an angry gorilla that was denied his second bucket of snacks—though I can't exactly say that was surprising coming from a mentally-unstable maniac holding a gun. "Hey, do-do-do y-you know how many times I had to rehearse this speech? I-I-I have a speech impediment; this took me months to perfect. If you don't at least pretend to care about this, I will—"

"What? Kill me?" I said, interrupting him in mid-sentence. Just because I might end up decorating the pavement and road below with my internal organs, it doesn't mean I can't be a smartass. "Why did you even bother to practice this speech anyway? It's not like you're going to have many opportunities to use it. To be honest, there can't be that many people out there who would bother listening to your speeches. I would rather jump off the ledge of this building than listen to another string of clichés that come through the black hole that you call your mouth. And I can think of a few things that I would much rather sit through, like four hours of truck commercials, a courtroom audio-visual recording of two lawyers bickering over the legal definition of negligence during a case of some old lady's pet dog dying inside a dog kennel for a hereditary disease caused by aggressive inbreeding compounded by severe allergies that wasn't part of the explicit instructions given to the employees handling the case, and yes, that lady was my grandmother and she loved her pet pooch Ruffles, and about three politicians' worth of family-values rhetoric."

His face reddened into that beautiful hue of red and purple people thought could only exist when an eggplant and a tomato had a baby. Well, the people thought wrong. "Why don't you just jump off the building then? I could just shoot you right now." He said, barely getting out the words in his rage. I can tell you that, in the twenty minutes that I have had the misfortune of truly knowing him, few people have ever had the guts to insult him and even fewer had the luck to survive such an encounter.

"What," I said, "And miss the chance of finally

getting to finish that speech you had been working so hard on for the last few months? Face it, you love yourself too much to settle for anything less than saying the whole thing. You would never be satisfied until you finished saying that terrible crime against humanity that you consider a speech. In comparison, the President of the United States sounds less self-absorbed than you, and that's a high bar to clear." By now, his forehead veins are sticking out like tree roots. Though I wouldn't exactly call myself a master of words, I secretly hoped for one of the veins to pop under the pressure and save me from the imminent death sentence that loomed in background and wrap everything up in a way would be more contrived and ridiculous than a desperate writer's attempt to ride on the coattails of other, much more successful, writers.

He struggled to contain his anger, but miraculously, he did somehow manage to get it under control just long enough to pretend to be intelligent again. "You may be right . . . I'll keep you around for another couple of minutes or so. But trust me, you will not be missed when that bullet slams into your head at point-blank distance!"

Was that meant to be a joke? I've seen punchline-delivery in an amateur boxing match, oh geez, if this dumbass was any worse at comedy, he would be writing Buzzfeed articles and contributing memes to 4chan. I've seen better wordplay from fourth-language speakers that have difficulty checking out books at the library, but even they would have made a much more intuitively funny witticism there because polyglots would be nothing if not clever with words.

Pity the next thing he's likely to crack is my skull instead of a witty one-liner.

Oh, who am I kidding? I was almost completely certain by then that I was going to survive this close encounter with the turd kind. Dying at the hands of someone whose idea of humour makes me imagine flies buzzing out of his mouth when he screeches out a shitty joke that butchers comedy so hard that it makes yo-mama jokes sound classy. Isn't denial a wonderful thing?

From the way things are going, I'm more likely to die of boredom than from a bullet to the head as I had originally assumed. His speech would never end if he insists upon stuttering through the whole thing and repeating each line until he enunciated them clearly, fill it with run-on sentence. He boasted of his non-existent oration skills (yes, within the same speech that he had been in the process of fucking up *with the intention of trying to intimidate* us) in such a way that if he gave me the gun, I might just shoot myself.

It was in that moment, a miracle has occurred—in the form of him finally finishing his goddamned speech. No, I'm not going to put you through the remainder of his speech, because his words are so irrelevant and disconnected that even Frankenstein's Monster would wince at how it was stitched together. Oh, that's right, this speech was written by a guy who probably failed English due to an inability to comprehend basic TEEL scaffolding. Though, unfortunately I didn't realise he finished his speech and I had decided to drag him down with me. It was only after it was too late did I realise that I could've averted this situation if I paid more attention. What could I say? I once accidentally 'liked' a xenophobic minion meme on Instagram posted by my aunt because I reflexively double-tap every image that comes into view to show that I've seen it. Is this the best way to deal with social media feeds? Probably not. Should I continue to do so? Maybe. Hotel? Trivago.

My life flashed before my eyes as I realised that I happened to still be alive. For some reason, he never did fire off his shot. Perhaps he realised just a little too late that maybe he forgot to pull the trigger or maybe the dog ate it, but that piece of information wouldn't have boosted my chances of survival at all. Falling from this height was still going to result in me being dead on the pavement, flat as a pancake (though I would be bringing someone else down with me). You don't need to know much human-approved high school physics to realise exactly how screwed you are on a scale of one to ten (hint: it's an eleven).

Now, how exactly did I end up in this mess? After all, it wasn't exactly the way I had pictured myself dying, and, by a ridiculous amount of misfortune, it seems like I might've died on a Monday. I *hate* Mondays, and the fact that my asshole boss Dick (his real name) is probably out there somewhere checking off an employee list to indicate that I haven't turned up for work for the fifteenth week in a row did not make Mondays any easier to tolerate . . . and that is if he hasn't already fired me already. Which is a very real possibility since I haven't turned up for work for so long that it would've made more sense to hire someone to replace me instead.

01

THE BEST PLACE TO START THIS STORY IS PROBABLY *the day after my friend 'died'.*

His name is not important, but you can call him Albest. He was kind of a weird person, like what would happen if you combined Neo from *The Matrix* with Austin Powers and filled in the gaps with a drug overdose. In other words, he stood on a fine line between pure stupidity and Keanu Reeves pretending to be a wooden mannequin (or is it the other way around?), and you couldn't tell whether he was a genuine asshole or just someone who was too honest for his own good . . . most of the time.

If divine providence existed in this world, Albest

would be what happened when one such being gave up on humanity and resorted to filling his entire personality with overused clichés and a Buzzfeed quiz for which *Supernatural* character he would be.

Albest earned a living by weaselling it from people with more money than sense—which usually happened to be the paranoid millionaire who wanted to keep tabs on their friend/spouse/mistress/cat. Trust me when I say that it was probably the best way to lose faith in humanity besides working as customer support while in high school. Given time, he might've become a drug addict from the sheer pressure that society forced upon him, but life didn't give him that chance. That was the day my life changed as well.

It was a rather anti-dramatic day, really. Everyone had more on their plates than they would care to admit to a casual stranger; after all, it was a weekday, and there's no rest for the damned (read: office employees). The police found him dead on a park bench with a syringe stuck in his arm while wearing duck flippers—which was weird, but also probably not the weirdest thing the police force had seen that morning; we *are* talking about the police, who responds to literally every phone call people make about emergencies, imagined or otherwise. Where we lived, there were angry kids who rushed onto counters at fast food restaurants in a temper tantrum because the shitty toys they got with their meals wasn't the ones they wanted. I had the luck of witnessing one such incident before, and the fact that the police managed to defuse the situation without making themselves look like idiots was quite amazing.

At the time, his supposed death was quite convincing and a rather nasty surprise for me; especially since I had received the news while I was on the toilet (the worst time to hear about the death of your best friend), not to mention the news was from my boss who happened to be the type of person that have no qualms about breaking that kind of news from another toilet cubicle). Again, it's not unusual for someone to die while on drugs; it happened every now and then, and Albest happened to be one of the few people who always looked high even when he wasn't. What truly pissed me off was how annoying my boss was. There I was, working minimum wage at a job that basically consumed my life, and that asshole slammed the door besides mine, let loose a Mt. Vesuvius, and then said something along the lines of, "Hey Peter, your friend's dead. Sorry 'bout that and all, but don't take the day off, okay? You're staying behind to finish the presentation for our next corporate meeting on Friday. My marriage depends on my ideas being cleared—heck, my salary depends on the idea being cleared. If I don't see the presentation ready in two days, you're fired." The worst part was that he didn't flush, and I saw the darkened porcelain shell stained with the stench of a farmhouse and all fifty shades of brown and red on my way to wash my hands. I made a point to alert the janitor as soon as possible.

Of course, my boss was a selfish asshole; though, being a sociopathic narcissist seemed to be part of the "boss package." I got the gist of it after watching about one seasons' worth of *Madmen*. Don't tell my mum that I never finished her favourite show.

I didn't realise back then that Albest wasn't dead and merely *faked* his own death, but that wasn't exactly the first thing that came to mind when I heard the news (my first thought after hearing this news happened to be: "Can I punch my boss and get away with asking for a day-off later?"); so imagine how surprised I was when a not-dead Albest called me that night.

I was tossing and turning in bed with all the vigorous motions of sex, but without the human part or, you know, the happiness. As I was contemplating sleep (that's right, contemplating, not actually sleeping), life intervened in the form of a ringing phone. Which is just the worst when little ol' me is struggling with insomnia. Thanks a lot.

I managed to knock over almost everything on my nightstand in order to pick up the phone with the unreasonable belief that it was my boss calling with a radically changed opinion (I really shouldn't have told him to go eat a dick when he rejected my application for a day off). Then I finally remembered that my phone was still inside my shirt because I forgot to take it out due to the fact that I had been drinking alcohol to escape from the depressing mess that was my life. I know, I know: alcohol on a weekday=bad idea. But hey, my best friend died, my boss was an asshole, and I was going to be doing unpaid overtime for the next two days. That should have been excuse enough for me to dig a hole and hide in it.

After some more fumbling, I picked up the phone and tried to sound professional. "Hello? You have reached Peter Stewart. Who is this?"

"This is me, Albest. I faked my death. Peter, I want you to come to my apartment right now. I apologise for making you worry about my death, but I have to go. They are coming. Your life's in danger." His voice sounded scratchy, and distant, hard to focus on; it was like trying to watch a movie while listening to static.

Of course, I tried to ignore the blatant pronoun

game he was playing and tried to concentrate on the phone call. "Is this a prank call? I just heard the news, like, a few hours ago? Isn't this a bit insensitive? I know he may be a douche. But can you try not to disturb my sleep?"

"Listen, brain-dead, I'm not dead. Also, do you really not recognise my voice? Someone is out to get you. Well, it might have been my fault, but the point is your life is danger, Pete."

"Oh," I said, as reality finally punched through my hazy wall of tiredness. Albest wasn't dead. Though it was mostly due to the fact that anyone else that dared to call me Pete had probably discovered that they might not survive the experience unscathed. "I thought you were dead, you prick. And it is way too early in the morning for this kind of— Albest? Hello?"

"Goddammit, even if he is alive. This usually isn't the kind of prank he'd normally pull," I half-grumbled to myself with gratuitous self-justification for why I'm doing this. I had dealt with his 'pranks' before, but nothing like this.

Since he hung up before I had time to talk and argue for the sake of it, I didn't really have much of a choice. I would visit that apartment Albest always told me about but never invited me to. To me, the place was almost as elusive and mythic as his 'girlfriend in Canada' and his 'pet that's living on a farm upstate'.

I didn't know what the flying fuck was going on, but I *did* know his address. *Only* the address—but that was definitely enough of a start. Feeling an odd burst of adrenaline, I suddenly felt awake, alert (though, it might have been the effects of the alcohol. I threw on some clothes and walked to his 'bachelor pad' with as much urgency as my alcohol-addled brain would let me without tripping over.

When I reached the apartment block, I stopped in my tracks and finally realised why Albest had never extended the invitation for me to crash at his place before.

The building loomed over the area, casting an eerie half-shadow as the gibbous moon shone down over me. Maybe it was just the odd moonlight and my alcohol-addled brain playing tricks on me, but I shivered as a chill crept down my spine. Something felt off about this creepy building. The place was silent. Deserted. Lacking even the sounds of crickets chirping in the background, with adjacent buildings just as deserted as the apartment looming before me.

The normal and urban appearances of this blasted place ought to have calmed and reassured me; but oddly enough, I only felt more disturbed as the road bumped and veered onward. At times it seemed as though every familiar aspect of the building was fresh and vague. I didn't feel secure; instead, I felt violated and harassed. Someone was watching me.

There was a strangely calming element of beauty in the landscape through, which was probably the only selling point of this dense location filled with deserted buildings and decaying shells. Time had lost itself in this labyrinths of decrepit, hollow, skeletons of once-ambitious architectural dreams. The lack of continuous funding and shady politics stopped the place from becoming a proper residential area.

I entered the building and my expectations were dashed even further. Imagine the dinkiest apartment you know, now add peeling paint, a sleeping security guard guarding precisely nothing, toppled trash cans, vandalised walls, and a torn notice board hanging on a nail covered in dust and grime. Congratulations, you've got a pretty good idea of what that place looked like.

After several futile attempts to wake the security guard, I gave up and ran towards a dangerous, rickety elevator. A gigantic cockroach scuttled in through an immense hole in the vent. I didn't even bother to be scared; I was already tired and whatever part of my brain that handles fear (it's the frontal lobe. Yeah, so what if I had once wanted to go to medical school and scouts, MUM? It isn't a nerd thing. That's what I meant when I said I wanted to be a doctor)—well, that part of my brain was asleep before I even got the chance to close my eyes.

I looked for signs of immediate danger such as broken pieces of wiring, faulty call buttons, any sign the elevator was going to kill me in the lamest way imaginable before actually going up to Albest's floor. As I travelled towards his floor, I endured whatever ungodly medley from the '70s era the elevator happened to be playing and successfully avoided dying with a cockroach by my side. As a personal rule, I would prefer to not die in the immediate vicinity of cockroaches.

When I had heard him bragging about the ultimate apartment that money could buy, I was in awe at his skill at finding whatever rathole that could technically pass as a 'living area'. After visiting this building . . . I was seriously wondering whether he was a closet masochist or not. The building looked like he had purposefully tried to—and succeeded—in finding the worst possible place to live in.

Yet his apartment was even worse than I imagined. The door was half-hanging off the frame, with at least one of the door hinges broken. That wasn't something that could be fixed. Albest needed to invest in a sturdier door frame and door hinges that didn't look older than my grandma. The doorknob was broken as well, though when door itself was barely hanging off the frames, the doorknob was unnecessary anyway. The lock was jammed with gum.

We always met either at my place or a café somewhere nearby; perhaps it was for the best. I would much rather live in my shitty house than accept oversized cockroaches as a part of my daily life (I had the misfortune of just sharing an elevator ride with one).

I pushed opened the door and, due to the fact that it was old and rusted, the hinges made a horrendous half-screeching cacophony.

As I stepped inside carefully, making sure not to break anything or accidentally step on a cockroach (I was especially wary of them after the aforementioned elevator ride), I surveyed the room. "Uh, Albest?" I said, not sure whether to whisper or yell.

The rational part of my brain then proceeded to tell me that this was a scam, since (as of that moment) I had met exactly zero people who had decided to fake their own death in any given situation.

As I called his name for the third time. "Albest!" Suddenly, a blurred figure flew out of nowhere and shoved me to the floor. Spine met wood and I made an embarrassing croaking sound. Without time to process what was happening, three successive gunshots rang out, sharp and focused. It was not the kind of noise you would expect from a normal gun; rather, the less-noisy sound of a sniper rifle.

A moment later, I was dragged into the master bedroom (Can you believe it? Albest actually had a bedroom! Well, it was the only one) and I took in the figure that had just saved me. He put a hand over my mouth before I could complain.

I realised that it was, in fact, my friend Albest who saved me from getting a bullet to the head as he took off his balaclava and tossed it away.

Albest placed a finger on his lip and that, as many should know, was a universal gesture for silence. So I quieted down and followed him. I mouthed to him whether or not he wanted to explain this to me later and whether or not I would get to punch him in the stomach for ruining my sleep schedule and nearly taking three bullets to my head. The only response I got was a grin that vaguely translated to a smug "screw you, I don't care."

I checked my surroundings and noted an obscene amount of newspaper clippings and tabloids covering the wall. Some of the clippings featured UFOs and a few others appeared to be internet printouts of extensive online forum discussions linked together via an obscene and offensively cliched amount of string. It looked less like a flowchart marked with string and more like a drug-addict's attempt to draw a metropolitan subway system.

The distant ping of an elevator sliding open rang off against the sound of silence. "Shit," I whispered. "You think maybe we should get out of here?"

In response, Albest lifted the bed up and pull open a hidden trapdoor. "Bolt for that trapdoor when the time is right," he whispered. "Our blood will be decorating these walls if you don't follow my instructions."

I waited for him to finish his preparation before saying, "Dude, too much melodrama." As he shoved a gigantic lump of machinery onto the trapdoor, one of the LEDs lit up green and it clicked open. The sound of footsteps grew louder and louder. It was headed our way.

"Go!" Albest said, and bolted inside with me following close behind. *So much for complicated instructions,* I thought as the trapdoor closed. Heavy thumping thundered on the other side. I flinched, catching my breath. The world was dark for a moment until the light turned on. Albest was way crazier than he had let on . . .

"I suppose I owe you an explanation," he said as we walked down and out of the dark passageway. Feeling like an idiot, I asked him to explain what the fuck was going on. As stress of recent events exploded within and I ranted for a couple of minutes. He smiled and explained the current situation.

"I faked my death," he said. "I bought some medicine off a really suspicious dark web auction site that can simulate a heart attack. When I say the website is suspicious, I mean, *really* suspicious. Like, Silk Road-level suspicious. I am about ninety-nine percent sure that the credit card I used had been leaked on the internet already. Good thing I didn't use *my* credit card. Ha. Ha . . . " He cleared his throat and continued. "After a while, I woke up in the morgue and had to call you to arrange a meeting in my apartment. As I stated in the phone call, I believe your life is in serious danger, and it may be my fault. Who knows? I haven't gotten all the facts on that one. Could be someone after your life. Things are in motion, my good friend. You would be correct to think that I don't have either money or patience to do anything like this. But I do have . . . friends that do happen to possess at least one of those things. They helped."

"There should be no reason why you needed to

plan and build a literal trapdoor connection to a secret passageway between the apartment walls. Why? Who did you piss off to elicit such a ridiculously strong reaction? No, wait, my biggest question is who gave you the rights to build this in the first place? This entire passageway feels like a building code violation, and I don't see how it could have been constructed unless it was pre-built into the build— Oh, so that's why you chose this shithole to live in."

"What can I say, the landlord was a serial killer—a rich one, too," Albest said, shrugging. "I suppose it's a bit unfortunate that he's an idiot who can't cover up his criminal predilections for shit. I uncovered his actions within days of moving into the damned place, and I blackmailed him into the prison system. In the meantime, I get to enjoy living in an apartment that has passageways connecting pretty much every part of the building together without ever needing to pay rent. Isn't this beautiful? The only investment I needed to make was constructing the trapdoor underneath my bed."

"Hey man, this isn't a movie, so please don't expect me to follow along like a clingy puppy until you have at least explained why the hell there are snipers outside who are trying to kill me. Who is inside the elevator? And when do I get to punch you in the jaw?" I asked, torrents of questions spewing out of my mouth.

"Don't worry. I will answer your questions once we're in a public place, like at that really downtrodden cafe filled with hoodie-wearing hipsters that are trying to write the next YA sensation on a MacBook Air or that shitty Mexican food place that served as PTSD material for the unfortunate food safety inspectors," Albest said evenly, expertly dodging my request of punching him by pivoting the subject to something unrelated. "I mean, there's also the Japanese restaurant ran by a Chinese family, but their cooking skills is average at best."

Well, sure, ignoring the fact that you're just answering whichever question is the least bothersome to answer and are purposefully withholding information that concerns my life, I thought as I got more and more pissed off at the fact that you're essentially demanding to go with the flow just because there's a sniper that seriously wants to kill me. *And also, man, that's some really harsh criticisms of the restaurants here. Did they really piss you off so much to the point that you're literally prioritising complaining about shitty restaurants over my life? Seriously, I haven't even gotten over the fact that you're supposed to be dead yet!*

"The explanation is going to be a bit long. But the long and short of it is that I took a really shady job and, somewhere in the middle of this bullshitty job, I got too involved with other people's secrets and voilà: assassins are dispatched to hide some secrets. They assume you know the truth too and now you're a target as well. Hahahaha." Albest started laughing mechanically. "That a good enough explanation? Hilarious. I know right? Who would be stupid enough to think I would share information with you?"

"Yes, that's a brilliant explanati—As if I would say something like that after all the shit that's happened! No matter how you look at it, it was you who purposely gave me an explanation that tells me nothing that I didn't already know or haven't already guessed except the fact that you're a bigger idiot than I thought. You woke me up in the middle of the night and almost got me killed by snipers that are stationed at *your bleeding apartment.* Give me a better explanation, dammit!" I seethed. Who knew what kind of attention I might've attracted if I started screaming? Did he get infected with the desire of schadenfreude when I wasn't watching? That asshole.

On that note, we walked at a brisk pace and swaggered out of an alleyway. I suspected that he had been intentionally vague just so he could tell a more dramatic story later. His answers left a lot of blanks that needed to be filled in.

He better have an actual explanation for all this, I thought.

02

AS WE WALKED TOWARDS THE SHOPPING DISTRICT, we entered a heated but decisive argument about which of the restaurants there was the lesser of the many evils (and also, where three out of five people would probably end up with food poisoning if they tried takeout).

Albest circled around the block to make sure we weren't being followed, but I wasn't as certain as he was that we were safe just yet.

About thirty minutes later—and that was thirty minutes longer than I had originally intended on arguing with him on the finer aspects of not getting poisoned with all the shitty chefs and ancient family restaurants operating around here—we decided on a suspicious Mexican food shop that was supposed to be run by a group of drug dealers . . . or so the rumour went. I didn't believe it. Even as a money laundering front this place seemed too surreal.

We ordered tacos (because that way we could actually see what they had put into said taco, and it was cheap) and then proceeded to sit in silence as we awaited the other person to start the conversation. It soon derailed into a mime involving many complicated gestures and even more awkward silences.

Great, I thought, *We will be stuck here all night waiting for someone to start the conversation at this rate.*

Albest opened his mouth to say something, but words failed to come out of his mouth (and yes, he looked very awkward and had the same facial expression you would generally make when you're trying to swallow an extremely large hot dog. <Insert generic penis joke over the usage of phallic symbolism here>). I don't know why, but it seemed like whenever things were difficult to explain, he lost his ability to speak. So, with no options left, I decided to talk first.

"Look, we are not going anywhere. The only reason I'm not leaving you is because of the explanation you promised me thirty-five minutes ago—and the fact you paid for the tacos. Now say something before I leave you here with the chemical weapon know as a 'shitty taco' and go to the nearest outdoor trekking store to buy a hunting knife that I could put under my pillow." I muttered, taking a bite of the damned taco and tried to think of something more pleasant, like the excretory wastes of the Human Centipede.

"Really? With your physical prowess, I would reckon you have a higher chance of stabbing yourself in the arm than actually protecting yourself from dangers with a hunting knife." Albest said, he took a deep breath and spoke steadily. "Okay, so this all started about seven months ago, when I got bore—I mean, when I found a job online. And, well, when I was browsing conspiracy sites— Ahem, I mean, *job-finding* sites, I came across a strange request to investigate the legitimacy of a government cover-up of a UFO landing. Which totally isn't suspicious at all and I totally didn't do this just because I was bored."

Albest, if you're going to lie about how much you hate work, please at least try and stop yourself from saying lazy lines like browsing conspiracy theory forums for shits and giggles, I thought to myself tiredly. I swear, if I didn't have better self-control and discipline, I might've actually said my inner monologue out loud. That was so close to slipping out.

"So, after a long investigation that actually required me to get off my ass and meet other people, I managed to confirm the legitimacy of the government cover-up. Because of this, I started stalking— Ahem, I mean, investigating the personal background of my client . . . Oh my god, it actually made me sound professional when I said the word 'client.' Don't judge; it isn't me being a creepy stalker as long as I have a good reason." Albest was grinning like a discount jack-o-lantern that you bought three Halloweens ago. Did I mention how annoying that grin was? It was the kind of smile that wordlessly promised a YouTube fail compilation of the things you did while drunk with a complementary "ahahaha, get fucked!" attached. That happened way too many times.

"Albest, have you ever wondered why no company has ever offered you a job? Yeah, I haven't either," I said, looking at Albest with my full attention. I really didn't want to believe this government conspiracy bullcrap involving aliens—especially the alien part. But even the craziest of theories could sound convincing if just forty-nine minutes ago, one had a narrow encounter with death. A few minutes more, and I might have gotten Death's phone number, too. Having dodged a literal bullet could be quite healthy for your scepticism and definitely leave you more attentive when someone explained why said bullet was aimed at you. "Alright," I said, "so what's the name of this conspiracy?"

His smile faltered slightly. "Sorry?"

"Ahem. The name of the conspiracy. All good conspiracy theories have good names, like the Illuminati files, or Moon Landings Uncovered, or Watergate. What's the conspiracy theory/scandal/thingymajig called?"

"Uhh ... Aliengate?" Albest said with a questioning voice that sounded way too uncertain.

"You just made that up on the spot, didn't you?" I said in resignation.

"Well whatever, the name's not important. Imma continue with my story here. Turns out that my client was a college student studying politics. That unlucky dude had an influential dad who knew some freaky shit about the government, which I found out after digging through his garbage. Aliens arrived in the equation shortly after as some ... *things* happened. Crazy? Yes. Improbable? No. Hotel? Trivago," Albest ranted madly, grinning with the ferocity of a jack-o-lantern overdosing on caffeine. I wasn't quite convinced that the conspiracy was as overarching and crazy as he said it was; though, this *was* the guy who shamelessly sent a bag of dildos to his best friend on a certain April fools' day using my credit card. To this day, I still don't know how he did it, nor do I really want to know. I did, however, change my credit card password.

"And can you explain to me exactly what 'things' happened to result in this situation?" I asked, gulping down the glass of water to distract myself from the current situation, and accidentally choked on the water.

"Well, I don't want to talk about it, but it does have something to do with the fact that there are aliens on Earth. And, no, by aliens I'm not talking illegal immigrants either . . . Well, okay, the immigrants of the *outer space* kind. 'Na mean?'"

Albest sneakily dodged the question yet again. With amazing ability to give only the vaguest answers, creating bullshit seemingly out of thin air, and instantly changing the topic in the blink of an eye . . . He could've become an excellent politician.

"I was onto something big," he said. "And I became a big, fat target. I think that's about it."

I sensed that Albest was about to say something more, but he suddenly stopped. His eyes had focused on someone else.

At first, I assumed that he was just checking out the waitress behind us serving table eight (because he was that kind of guy). However, I realised that something wasn't quite right. He looked absolutely terrified. There wasn't much that could scare Albest.

"Albest, what's wrong and what in the seven hells is frightening you so much to the point that you look like you might wet your pants? Albest? Hello? Earth to Albest? If there is something you need to tell me . . . tell me right the hell now or I'll splash this small glass of cold water onto your face." I grabbed the glass of water in preparation.

That brought him back to focus, but he didn't crack a smile, so I decided that it had nothing to do with the bored-looking waitress behind us. The waitress gave us a dirty look that was the waitress equivalent of giving us the finger.

"The old man sitting behind us at table eight hasn't ordered anything in the time we've been here," Albest said. "And no, the waitress refilling his water bottle doesn't count as ordering anything. He is reading a month-old newspaper with about as much interest as I would with a cars magazine. And he is— Oh shit. Run."

Right on cue, everyone in the restaurant except us (which was about . . . seven people) screamed and ducked behind or under whatever they had decided could offer them protection. The staff moved into the kitchen like this was something that had been covered in their training manual (and I could totally imagine the restaurants in the neighbourhood doing something to that effect given how shady the whole place was). The old man (middle age was closer to the mark than old age) that Albest had been ogling stood up with vigour and urgent purpose as though someone had shoved a needle up his ass. Dropping the newspaper, he pulled out a gun from . . . somewhere within his trousers. Dear god, someone introduce him to a holster.

He pulled the trigger.

In that one terrifying, confusing moment, I stopped reacting just as Albest scrambled under the table and threw me out the window using the momentum from his fall.

FYI: being thrown through a window hurts, but not as much as being hit by a bullet. I wasn't hit, so that was good, I suppose.

I tripped and landed on my knee outside. Numerous ways to verbally express my pain popped into my mind but I gritted my teeth to lock them in.

As I scrambled towards my house, I ducked and swooped with a bounce, as though doing this would somehow increase my chance of survival. Within moments, louder sounds erupted behind me, and

Albest caught up with me, running with just as much fervour. Panicked, I faced forward and continued to run as fast as I could towards my house.

. . . and then it exploded.

03

NOW, AS A GENERAL POINT OF REFERENCE, I SHOULD mention that I liked my house and was yet to pay off the mortgage for it. And I wasn't quite sure how much the insurance company would cover for an attempted murder attempt via bombing. I wondered how much money I had on myself in that moment. I probably wasn't getting any more out of that house. Boo.

All of that flashed through my mind at the precise moment I saw my house go up in flames. I shouldn't have been so attached to a house, but it was a huge investment, dammit. Watching my hopes and dreams explode like an old, flammable piñata had a big emotional impact on me. That came as a hard blow to the nuts and, more importantly, my wallet.

I turned around to face Albest, wearing a flat mask of calm on my face. I tried my best to forget about the pathetic collection of tacky medals my boss gave me for 'the most boring office cubicle of the year' for three years running, my manly dreams (read: fetish porn) stored on the now-unrecoverable hard drives of my computer, and the ironic Mother's Day present that I never wrapped stashed under my bed with the many boxes of instant noodles.

Then I punched him in the face.

"You bleedin' asshole!" I shouted, consciously aware of the sleeping neighbours nearby. I didn't want to disturb them (though, the fact that they could sleep through an explosion should've told you all that you needed to know about them. They may have been heavy sleepers, but that was mainly because of the fact they were war vets).

"If you're going to involve me in a life-threatening government conspiracy, send an email first!" I said. "No, I don't care whether this shit is traceable, what I care about is if you know my house is going to be destroyed, tell me before it happens. I could've at least had the chance to back up my PC." I stared at him with simmering rage. I punched him again, he ducked out of range and threw on a sheepish smile.

"Wait, you *don't* habitually back up your PC?" he said, looking at me in surprise.

"Albest . . ." I waved my fists threateningly.

"Listen, I only found out that aliens are after your life, like, four hours ago," he said, moving away from to avoid another knuckle sandwich. "It was pretty much immediately after I woke up in the morgue. Even if I *had* sent an email, it probably would've landed in your spam folder anyway. There's really no better solution right now other than to follow me for a few weeks and hope it blows over really quickly. When this whole mess clears up, I promise I'll get you something good to compensate for the loss of your shitty house, as well as the weird fetish porn that's on your laptop."

"Hey!" I whispered. "Don't talk about fetish porn out loud. I will never live it down if someone overhears, you know?"

"Peter, it's literally three in the morning. The kinds of people that are still awake at this moment are too drunk to even remember how to properly tie their shoelaces. They aren't going remember two people slugging it out in front of the burnt remains of what used to be a house. That's just a normal weekday to them."

"Point taken. But I assure you, I'm perfectly normal. Thirteen hours ago, I was still worrying over contacting Bob from marketing to talk about how to best organise a PPT presentation that I was in charge of," I said, looking at him in exasperation.

At this point Albest grinned. "And tell me, precisely what kind of normal person ventures out at the dead of the night to his deceased friend's apartment just because of a vague phone call? And also, really, someone decided to put you in charge of organising the presentation for company meetings? Wow, and I thought you couldn't sink below minimum wage and being 'proficient in Microsoft Office.'"

My fists were begging me to sock Albest in the face again, but my saner side prevailed and reasoned that I would only look that much more of an idiot if I had to resort to violence to prove a point. "Well what kind of normal person browses conspiracy theory websites when they're supposed to be looking for a job and then drags their best friend into multiple life-threatening situations without even bothering to properly explain things?"

"Hey, Pete-y, I never claimed that I was a boring little office joe like you." He grunted. Obviously not wanting to pursue that train of thought, he said, "Look, I know a place that isn't burnt ashes and melted plastic. I would say it's pretty safe for a temporary hideout. So, do you mind being quiet for a while and following me to my car? Distracting the driver would really not be beneficial to the passenger."

I snorted, but kept my mouth shut and continued to follow him. A friend of mine once gave me a piece of advice that led me through *many* stressful company interviews and similarly stressful situations: When you don't know shit, follow the people that actually know what they're doing. That piece of advice had never failed me. I didn't see any reason why it would fail me in that situation, either.

As I climbed into the car, Albest decided to start it up without any warning or consideration to the passenger (me). Now, common logic would tell you that if you expected things to be smooth sailing from that point on despite having been previously assaulted by snipers, having your house blown up, and being dragged into a grand conspiracy that would very likely take your life . . . then you were stupid or very optimistic.

About ten minutes after I jumped into Albest's car, gunshots started firing at us, the windshield started sporting bullet holes and three Biker-gang-wannabes started circling us like a carousel of dicks. The Harley Davidson and the smoking guns they held in their hands indicated that we might be in a spot of trouble.

I dodged down and painfully bent my neck at ninety degrees so as to avoid the barrage. "Remind me again, why is it that there are *always* murderous people behind us and why don't they have futuristic ray guns? According to the pattern here, wouldn't it make more sense that, if aliens and their cronies were pursuing us, they would be holding ray guns or some other futuristic bullshit?"

"Well, the aliens use their super-advanced futuristic technological BS as a bartering chip to gain political power. No one in their right mind would want to follow a group of mysterious aliens and just hand them control over the world if they didn't have something to gain from it. Because of that, they keep their advanced technology close to the chest, otherwise they would lose their chance of gaining political power in the background, after all, there is only so much liquid gold to piss out when you're all King Midas up in this shit." Albest grunted, ignoring the gunshots behind us, swerving dangerously every now and then.

"HOW DOES THAT ANALOGY MAKE ANY KIND OF SENSE?" I shouted from my cover.

"IT DOESN'T HAVE TO, AND WHY ARE WE SHOUTING!!??" Albest screamed over the sounds of bullets zipping past.

I rolled my eyes and stayed silent.

"The gentlemen behind us will give up soon enough. Unlike what movies would tell you, high speed car-chases are *never* practical and, while this isn't a bullet-proof car, our odds of being hit are pretty low. Look, it's obvious they can't aim for shit, not to mention I'm a good getaway driver." He signed, and started giving out exposition while maintaining a calm air of indifference, as though that part about being a getaway driver had some truth and experience backing it.

Red light. Albest slammed the brakes.

"Uh, why did you stop the car?" I asked.

"Because there's a red light, and I don't particularly want to get pulled over by the coppers unless I really have to." Albest explained. "Oh, don't worry about the people chasing us, they're about two streets behind and we'll be outta here before the sun's up. I know a place where we can go."

"That wasn't what I was asking," I said, with a slight feeling of irritation building up in my chest.

Albest laughed, and a dark sense of foreboding slapped me in the face. Whenever he laughed like that, it meant somebody was about to get screwed over. That was one consistency throughout the years I had known him. "Peter, are you perhaps a little bit disappointed that you didn't get to experience a movie-like car chase? Well then, it's as they say: there's no time like the present."

Then I started screaming.

04

LOOKING BACK, FOLLOWING ALBEST WAS PROBABLY the biggest mistake I have ever made in my life. And, unless I happened to receive *another* phone call in the middle of the night detailing my impending death, then this would probably *cement* itself as the worst decision of my life.

It really wasn't the best idea to trust the driving skills of a man who took six tries to get his license and still drove like an angry drunk. I regretted even *implying* the mere thought that I had never gotten the chance to experience a car chase . . . and after that I never wanted to experience it again. Even if you were an atheist, I believe that just by being a passenger in

Albest's car would make you find faith in God and the afterlife. It is an acceptable outcome of the worst possible situation.

As the worst two hours of my life sped by, I clung desperately onto the seat in front of me like a drowning man would cling to a plank of wood in the ocean. The car swerved dangerously from one lane to another with all the precise driving skills of an angry hamster, and I swore with the broad vocabulary of an angry office worker who was in the process of regretting every single life decision that he had ever made. I didn't know where the hell I was headed but, as long as it wasn't the afterlife, it was better than here.

Trusting a man who was reckless by nature and a shitty driver by habit was something that no one should ever do under any circumstance. I think I'd take being shot to death over being a passenger when Albest was behind the wheel. I do know for a fact that I would much rather have Lady Luck take the wheel than let Albest within a three-metre radius of another car.

Before long, we stopped at a small library just outside the town and I breathed a heavy sigh of relief, somehow having survived the treacherous journey. I didn't think I would ever be able to survive being stuck in the middle of an alien conspiracy with a 'friend' who was about as reliable as Costco's customer service, especially not when spending two hours in a car with him amounted to more life-threatening situations than I had experienced in my entire life. And, if being placed in as many life-threatening situations by a guy who is trying to protect you from other life-threatening situations isn't ironic, then I seriously couldn't tell you what is.

Albest stretched a bit before announcing, "This is the place. Welcome to my current home. It's not much, but I'm not exactly going to complain."

I said nothing; I was still recovering from the shock of seeing the license plate of a gigantic truck come up less than half a meter away from our car. I wanted to applaud myself for not curling into a tiny ball right there and then. I was still alive after that ordeal and, considering Albest's track record, I should've been thankful that I wasn't dead or in a coma.

We stopped in front of the public library. It was a sad shell of a building that once had bright walls and beautiful illustrated sign hanging at the top of the entrance. To put it in no uncertain terms, it was once a wonderful place, now it is just a depressing reminder of what once was.

Now, its paint had been peeled off, the elegant

sign at the top was missing half of its letters, and the door had obscene suggestions that really shouldn't belong on a library door graffitied onto it. The path was covered with lichen growing through the cracks and dried cement, indicating a historical attempt at the modernisation of our once-symbol of local pride.

Underfunded and fallen into disrepair were the first few words that popped into my mind as I took in this somewhat sad sight of a library that suffered severe underfunding after its budget was slashed to support the construction of a public museum of arts for . . . some reason. The town never really had many renowned artists, and the few talented artists that I happened to know had now turned to drawing furry and inflation porn for three thousand bucks per commission ("Artistic integrity? Dignity? What's that? Can you eat it?" – a depressed digital artist that used to own a nice house) . . . those artworks belong in a *different* kind of museum. Our town couldn't afford renaissance paintings anyways—other museums wouldn't part with their collections even if you held their mothers for ransom. So, all in all, our town was sparsely populated with tone-deaf attempts at modernisation and renovations that no one asked for nor needed while nearby companies herd their workforce like cattle and commit all the residents here to a slow and painful death by gentrification in an already-dead town.

I said nothing, again. There was really no appropriate way to react to the news that I would now be living inside this ancient rotting building situated at the farthest edge of town.

I followed Albest inside, past the flickering lighting that barely illuminated the dark entrance, past the empty shelves of the children's books section, past the fiction section, and beyond the self-help section not far away and into the . . . disabled toilet.

"Wait, what? I exclaimed in shock. Living a thrifty life inside a library might be a bookworm's romance, but living inside a spacious toilet was a homeless man's desperate cry for help. It did not help that said toilet was inside a library that was recently sued after a small group of cockroaches and rats were discovered in its dark corners (And yes, it was closed down at the time, and it was sued by thieves that intended to steal the windows . . . Don't ask). In an unsurprising turn of events that surprised absolutely no one, the library caved and was forced to eke out a settlement that cost them their hope of ever reviving this library from with the support of the regional representatives.

"Hey, I did say it's not much." Albest shrugged,

flicking off an unidentifiable slime-like thing that was stuck on the soles of his shoe with the tip of his fingers, then proceeding to wash his hands in the sink. "But at least it has running water, space, a toilet and even a shower for some reason. It's better than most shady apartments."

"Yeeah, sure. You did say that. I guess my expectations were set a bit high after discovering that you had enough money to install a secret exit into your apartment. A bat-cave with a charming British butler would be nice." I laughed dryly and started to try to brainwash myself into believing that this was really not as bad as it looked. Had my expectations been slightly corrupted by watching too many thriller films? Maybe. Following the pattern that would lay out for us, wouldn't this be roughly the moment where I would follow Albest into some seedy Fight-club like place, get introduced to some ragtag group of rich people who *weren't* into aliens, then get a few good layers of plot armour slapped on, arm ourselves with some futuristic weapons as we lead the Resistance after gaining a grudging respect from the initially indifferent group of jaded Resistance vets and charge into a panoramic panning shot of action? Was it too much to expect this malfunctioning toilet to, in fact, be a fancy secret hideout like the kind you saw in MIB? You know, the ones with a shit-ton of holograms and phaser guns or whatchamacallits?

"You can put your stuff on the diaper changing stati–"

"No. Don't suggest that idea again. My only good set of clothing that isn't burned in the explosion that took out my house is not about to smell like baby poop," I said, glaring at Albest. I basically had nothing on me besides my phone, a small wallet, and keys that officially opened nothing because my house exploded. Things . . . really weren't looking good. At least my phone had full battery—but even that was headed for the red zone in a few days.

Albest sighed deeply. "I'm pretty sure the cleaners disinfected these areas before leaving. They may be incompetent, but at least they're aware of basic hygiene rules and aren't stripped of their humanity. Besides, if you're really that worried, use the wet tissue wipes. Sure, they are dry now, but they'll be wet tissue wipes once more if you rinse it out with water. Just put your stuff somewhere first, so you don't have to sleep with your phone in your pocket. That'll feel very uncomfortable and you might crush your phone in the process. That'll suck.

"Though, I don't have a spare sleeping bag prepared for you because of the whole last-minute-discovery-of-bomb-planted-in-your-house thing my friend just found out in the nick of time. I was no less surprised than you were when the news got to me," Albest continued, rambling on and on as though there was no tomorrow. In a movie, he would be the underpaid disposable guy whose only purpose was to deliver exposition. "You see that shower area over there? Yeah, you can sleep there. Don't worry, I'll take down the shower curtains and give it to you to use as blankets. I think I also have some chocolate bars stashed inside my backpack. You are free take a few if it helps you to calm down."

That was a low point in my life. Sleeping inside a spacious toilet with showering curtains as blankets, I'd be crying if it weren't for the fact my best friend was behind me whistling to the tune of the *Yellow submarine*. Well, I tried my best to get over it and started making my temporary 'bed' as comfy as possible.

I stretched out my arms and ran out of the disabled toilet. I felt like I would go insane if I had to stay in that place any longer. Albest was the kind of guy who was always in your face, and this library, to me, felt like a testament to degradation. I didn't feel reassured, nor did I feel safe.

The famous invention called the book was, as

always, the best companion for the lonely hobo. It was a source of comfort for those in need. Maybe a light-hearted, science-fiction story with shooting, guns, and whimsical aliens set in the modern world would lighten me up. I knew a few authors that wrote stories like that.

The floors creaked as I exerted my weight upon it, aged wooden planks poking upwards. *They really need to replace these floorboards,* I thought, *as with most of the library.*

I trudged onwards, careful not to step on any of the rotted planks; the probability of the floor shattering under my weight was an uncomfortably real possibility of what would happen next with how aged this place was. Some buildings age like fine wine; others age like sour milk.

Sounds reverberated with resounding volume as I walked. At one point, I realised that I wasn't making these noises. I stopped moving, and listened.

Snores emanated from the Children's Books Section, a dull, tinny sound that I could've ignored, but my curiosity pushed me onwards.

Now, I wasn't gonna be scared of any random noises, but after the shit I had been through up until that point . . . I figured I was allowed to feel anxious at random noises.

I half-tiptoed towards that area. I peered over the shelves to spy upon the source of those sounds. Curiosity killed the cat, and we all know why curiosity killed the cat, now, don't we?

In the middle of the room, on one of the disparate series of couches, a woman slept. A stack of books and a bag of takeaway food could be spied being placed by the side. I walked closer and asked, "Umm, hello?"

"Ahhh!" the woman screamed, *politely*, as all normal people would inside a library. I rattled backwards. Not anticipating the panicked response. We both calmed down after a few seconds passed. I suppose this could be a normal response towards a stranger waking you up in the middle of the night. I'm certain that I would be prone to such actions as well.

The woman squinted her eyes at me, looking at me with as much seriousness as she could muster having just woken up. "Who the fuck are you, man? And why are you inside a closed library in the middle of the night?" I coughed. "Ahem. Generally, people introduce themselves first before asking for other people's names, and I would like to ask you the same question. I don't suppose you snuck in for a good night of reading, did you?"

The woman snorted, her hands darting into the

pockets of her jacket—where I glimpsed the faintest outline of a weapon. "What makes you so sure I'm not here to read books? I came here to read, and I just happened to . . . feel a bit drowsy. So what?"

But of course, Albest dived in at that moment, thankfully dissolving the awkward tension that was forming. He must've rushed here after hearing the scream. He stopped when he saw the woman and asked quizzically, "Peter, what that noi— Jane? Why are you here?"

Jane looked at him with a complicated expression. "I work here, you idiot. If I'm not here, where the hell would I be?"

"Yeah well, this place closed down ages ago. Anyways, I thought you went to work at a bookstore or something, anyways, you didn't mention you were coming in the phone call." He continued talking. Obviously, he knew the woman.

I glanced at the two of them. "I take it you guys are acquainted? You guys mind tellin' me what's going on right now? I feel like there's something complicated going on 'tween you two."

Albest coughed. "Well, remember back a few years ago when I 'accidentally' made one of the toilets in the library overflow because I was playing with a bunch of chemicals and clogged up the pipes?"

I nodded. "Yeah, and I remember you appearing on TV shouting that you were innocent, and that it was a misunderstanding."

After hearing that, Albest wore an expression that looked like he had a cockroach stuck in his throat that he couldn't quite cough out. "Well, those were the days. Anyways, to make a long story short, that's basically about the time I met her. Her name's Jane."

". . . Right," I said dryly. "How does that relate to our current situation? Don't tell me her house also exploded."

I was met with an awkward silence. Albest and Jane exchanged a brief glance and apparently reached some sort of mutual understanding.

"Wait, that didn't actually happen, did it?" I said nervously. Awkward silences generally meant that there was an answer that someone didn't want to say.

"Sorry to disappoint you, Mr . . ."

"Peter. Peter Stewart." Dammit, I thought I'd already introduced myself a few times. Was my name really that hard to remember?

"Well, sorry to disappoint you, Mr Peter. But my house didn't explode or suffer any actual damage. It's just that after I ended up seeing some things I shouldn't see, I ended up receiving some threatening messages placed inside my car via carrier pidgeon, and those bastards all shat on the bonnet of my car. Then I escaped a few attempted poisonings," Jane said, with the light touch of a pseudo-British accent that I couldn't quite place down to the exact location, and described her experiences with the same nonchalant air of someone who was describing her morning routing instead of terrifying assassination attempts.

"Actually, there was a guy as well, wasn't there? There was a guy who shat on your car as well, plopped down a right old—" Albest murmured, thinking about something absent-mindedly.

"Don't, get started on that please. That somehow the weirdest and the worst thing out of a whole slew of assassination and defamation attempts." Jane said wincing.

"Anyways, back to the main topic at hand, I went to her place and explained to her about the whole alien conspiracy when I realised they were after her," Albest said slowly with a tight expression that told me Jane hadn't quite taken his charismatic explanation as well as I had. "It was totally unrelated to your house exploding, by the way."

"Anyways, shit happened," Jane said. "We parted ways a few weeks back. And then an . . . acquaintance told me that a friend of Albest's might be in danger.

We exchanged a phone call, and then I rushed over." Jane rubbed her forehead as she spoke, as if remembering an unpleasant situation before quickly adding, "Oh yeah, and Albest just hung up without saying anything. So I rushed over to see whether the guy was alive, and I bought takeout."

An awkward silence followed as Jane stared at Albest accusingly. In turn, Albest looked like he was trying his best think of literally any other conversation to have except this.

Albest laughed nervously without humour. "Now, I know how this sounds but—"

"Okay, I get the gist of the story," I said. "So . . . basically you guys met a long time ago, and Albest got his ass stuck inside a stupid government conspiracy involving aliens and you guys met again after finding out that both of you were somehow stupid enough to become involved in a crazy government conspiracy. Involving aliens. Aliengate. Ugh, I can't believe I'm saying that stupid name. Afterwards, that asshole standing over there dragged *me* into it as well after you told him my life was in danger. Did I get everything right?"

Albest nodded, basically confirming my fears of being in a situation that was the equivalent of being trapped on a sinking boat with drunk sailors and a few empty buckets. Accepting the worst-case scenario, I bravely made eye contact with Albest and stared.

A tiny breeze blew through the room . . .

A tiny breeze blew through the room again . . .

A tiny br—

"Peter, are you going to say something or not?" Albest snapped. "You've been staring at me for more than a minute already! This isn't a shitty romance novel! We don't sell that shit here."

I broke eye contact with Albest and focused back on the situation. "Heheh, sorry but I was just going to call it a night and get a book to read as I go to sleep. Then I saw Jane sleeping on the couch o'er there. Everything can be discussed tomorrow after I wake up. Say, Jane, can you recommend any good science fiction stories to fall asleep to? Preferably the type that are slow, boring, and written by an immature idiot who doesn't even know a single thing about writing?"

"Oh sure, there are plenty of them in the Adult fiction area. There are a few that I personally recommend in the L section, but I suppose you might want to check out the browsing section as well; the books there all happen to fit your criteria and they are *terribly* boring . . . " Her voice trailed off as she led me towards the fiction area to pick out a book of my choice. Albest didn't follow after us, he snorted derisively at my literary tastes and returned to his toilet.

After finding a suitably boring book filled with purple prose, stilted dialogue, and shitty characters living in a shitty world, I read a few pages of the story and immediately fell asleep as blissful tiredness overtook me.

05

SCREAMING AT THE TOP OF MY LUNGS WITH RIVULETS
of sweat pouring down my face, I woke up. Reality
crashed into me with the force of a ten-ton truck. It
was a dream. Goddamn, but I hadn't had dreams that
messed up since finishing high school. Back then, I
at least had the excuse of blaming puberty, but now?
Yeah, I had no excuses.

Albest was fitting a silencer onto a pistol when
I woke up. He jolted and tightened his grip around
the trigger in accident because of my screams. As I
screamed at the top of my lungs, a shot rang out.

The bullet ricocheted around the room and grazed
Jane on the shoulder.

"Ow! Albest, ya fucking ass-wipe! Did you do that on purpose?" She looked at him angrily, and proceeded to give him a one-sided lecture on the merits of safe gun usage and the value of flicking on the safety in a crowded area.

It was only after what felt like an entire hour has passed during which Jane had berated Albest for his actions, that he had the chance to talk to me about my morning. He looked grumpy, and that was partially my fault.

"Rough night?" he said, scowling at me.

"Yeah," I admitted. "Had some fucked-up dream. And the hangover's still giving me a headache. It's pretty bad. Sorry for messing up your morning, eh? At least you didn't kill anyone. That's good."

He sighed, then went back to cleaning his pistols and stuff, rubbing the same spot over and over again. Loading bullets, cleaning guns and all that jazz. Dunno how that worked, but it looked neat.

"What's the point of these guns?" I asked stupidly.

I'll save you the pain of me raving on about how Albest then looked at me with a unique mixture of scorn, pity, and a condescending smile.

Albest opened his mouth and said, "Well, I need to protect myself from being killed. What can I say, I don't wanna die just yet. I love this gun, and you know what? The only way to stop a bad guy with a gun is a good guy with a gun. I'm taking this with me and I sure as hell am going to use it later and shoot out a whole steaming heap of foreshadowing. Every main character that have a cinematic fight scene in movies have glamorous-as-fuck guns that are shiny and sexy."

"Huh," I said, pretending to be interested, and furrowed my eyebrows in thought. "I recently watched a documentary on how smuggling arms past the borders is becoming harder than ever because of the increasing numbers of terrorist groups and recent shootings. Aren't guns bad?"

Albest snorted, as though he was looking down on me for semi-quoting facts from a documentary that I barely remembered watching. "Well, that's an entirely different argument for a situation found in an entirely different context, Peter. How are we the bad guys? We should probably use guns and *have* guns, goddammit."

"Wow. Everything in that sentence was wrong." Jane rolled her eyes and glared at Albest. "How much help has your cutesy gun been so far? *None*. You can't carry that thing on the streets, and you can't aim those things with precision either. Don't brag about your extensive knowledge of guns. I know you pretty well, and I can guarantee that you know guns as much as you know the Dewy Decimal System. In other words, I'm saying you don't know shit. You spent three months googling YouTube videos that teach you how to assemble firearms and look cool. For heavens' sake, you aren't even licensed to own a gun, much less shoot one. To this day, you still can't even flick the safety on and off without me reminding you how to." She paused. "Come on, we have go."

With that, Jane grabbed her bag and left the room. Confused, I asked Albest where we were going. Albest looked at me with a complicated expression before answering, "You don't expect us to hole up in this library for the rest of our life, do you? You have your whole life ahead of you as the world's most boring office worker ever working a vague job inside a mind-bogglingly large corporate hierarchy that I neither understand nor care about, and why would we ever let you sacrifice that honourable title just because of a crazy conspiracy? Come on, we're going to meet some people, get breakfast, and hopefully things will end up like a stereotypical fairy tale where you get your house back and everyone lives happily ever after."

"Albest, can you try and not act like an asshole for, like, five minutes?" I threw my hands up in resignation. Sure, being an office worker wasn't exactly a fantastic job, but at least it paid well and gave me a stable income. Even office workers had pride, you know? At least we office workers had a spine, unlike politicians and political news readers.

Albest chuckled nonchalantly, before gesturing me to follow him out of the library and into the parking lot. I complied, of course, and was then almost immediately greeted with the sight of the goddamned car I rode in last night (you start to develop an unreasonable hatred for a specific car when the driver of said car drives like a maniac while you're the passenger) and a minivan. It didn't take a genius to figure out who owned the mysterious minivan (especially as there were only two vehicles here in the entire parking lot).

"Why do you drive a minivan?" I turned towards Jane, who was fishing for her car keys from her bag, and asked quizzically.

"Why shouldn't I? The library is basically one signed document away from being knocked down. The books have to go *somewhere*, don't they? They can't just decompose inside the library with no one reading them. Books exists to be read, shared, and enjoyed; they don't deserve to die inside a decaying library that's only a shadow of what it once was."

Albest rolled his eyes at her, inciting a heated debate between the two on the merits of books.

"Fair point." I shrugged, and hesitantly walked towards Jane's car, I am not going to step inside his car ever again. Glancing at Albest with a subtle hint of pleading in my eyes to gain a clue of where I was being led to. Since I had no idea what the fuck was going on the whole time, I thought I was owned at least a brief explanation of the big plan here. Unfortunately, due to my nervousness and Albest ending up being (unsurprisingly) an extremely uncooperative douche, he patted my shoulder very heavily and instead said, "It okay. Jane's driving. We're ditching my car here. Go on."

I was half-shoved into the minivan. They failed to give an explanation of any kind. After about fifteen minutes of driving, we stopped at a gas station and bought breakfast. Vegan Muffins, vegan coffee (that's an actual thing), and some veggie bars. So that was good. At least I could inject a healthy diet into myself. If it were Albest calling the shots, he'd probably drive to the nearest Mexican food parlour and then order a messy burrito for everyone—which was one of the reasons I couldn't stand him. Thankfully, Jane was not only a good driver, but someone who enjoys a select sort of healthy food that I'm sure everyone could agree with.

It wasn't until I couldn't see the library through the rear window anymore that I finally gathered up the courage to ask him the big question. "Albest, where are we going?"

"We're going to a place where most of your problems will be solved. And all shall be revealed in due time," Albest said mysteriously with a slight hint of smugness in his voice, having taken up the ancient duty of providing (and dragging out) exposition as a Gandalf-like character with sadistic joy . . . and let's not mention how it was absolutely *typical* of these characters to have an aversion to practicality. I furrowed my brows in annoyance. I disliked the vague fuck-you that Albest had kindly sent my way, but I knew better than to question him now. Last year, when I asked him what Christmas present he was planning to give me, I never managed to pry anything more detailed than a brand name out of his mouth before he gave me the present. If Albest doesn't want to tell you something, then you can't get him to tell you. No amount of chocolates and sweets could bribe him to loosen his lips. Trying would just be a waste of time and I really disliked wasting anything.

When night fell, a gigantic interconnected

structure of several parking lots and multi-layered buildings was revealed before me. It was a post-modernist style building that held the proud title of being the lifeline of modern tourism, business transactions, and long-distance travel. For you see, it was—

"—Really? An airport?" I complained to Albest, exasperated with his stubbornness to reveal where we were going. I felt like I was being kidnapped. Not knowing where you're going whilst trapped inside a dinky minivan that smelled of old books and coffee incited those feelings in you. "When the hell did you order plane tickets for us? I thought plane tickets are things that you have to order in advance and need IDs and visas and stuff. How the hell did you do it?"

Albest shrugged, seemingly bored as he expressionlessly handed me a fake driver's license. "Well, remember that acquaintance Jane and I share? That guy sorted stuff out. Great person. I would give him a five-star *Yelp!* review if I could. We're going to check in and everything's going to turn out okay."

"You know how there's a group of disposable stock characters calling themselves the Resistance in the *Terminator* films, the *Matrix* and basically every other science fiction film slash novel where there's some kind of semi-omnipotent entity involved or a shadowy conspiracy spanning the globe?" Jane asked. "Well, basically that. But low budget. Anyways, I got a contact in there that'll help us out. His name is Wang Wu Er. I would vouch for his abilities in much the same way that I would vouch for the quality of any film starring Nicholas Cage and/or Tom Cruise."

I nodded. "So, I'm being taken to this . . . 'Resistance' to safely live out the rest of my life? Like those witness protection programs in the FBI?"

Albest threw a look of condescending pity at me. "Nah. If you really think things are going to be that easy, then you are about to be disappointed. They're an organisation that fights against alien influence, apparently. Those pompous douchebags think they are the other side of the coin of this whole 'Aliengate' conspiracy. They're not running a charity over there. I doubt they'd bother to help you get your life back together without having you cough out blood, sweat, and tears first."

I paused for a second before slowly starting to speak again. "Good point. There's no such thing as a free lunch in this world."

"Where did I put the flyer again? I was sure I put it inside one of my pockets. Did I lose it?" Albest grumbled, as he searched his pocket for a fat load of . . . nothing. He looked at his hand in surprise and searched his backpack for a while as he attempted to find the flyer.

Finally, he pulled out a crumpled tourist brochure advertising a plain city not far from where we were at the border. To be honest, though, this pathetic excuse of a city probably wasn't even worth the cash paid for the plane tickets. *Still better than the shithole town we live in, though.* I thought, absent-mindedly as I flicked through the flyer, feeling the bare minimum amount of awe.

"Here's the place we're going to," Albest said. "Hopefully things will go according to plan and nothing too bad will happen. I jotted down what I know about them, just so you know. But I don't really know much about those guys either. There weren't any traces of them that I could really investigate. And I didn't really have the time to do any of that last year, since I was a little busy running for my life and trying not to have my body chopped into tiny little pieces by fairly sadistic assassins that I am relatively sure would make great serial killers if they put their minds to it."

"*BREAKING NEWS!! DIRTY TERRORISTS BOMB TINY TOWN. MANY ESTIMATED DEATHS!! SATANIC RITUALLS INVOLVED!!??*" the airport newsfeed blared, with some of the screens being replaced with our faces and text. That was not good news. A picture of the smouldering ruins of my house was shown on the screen. I resisted the urge to continue to stare at the screen as one of the speakers continued to narrate the news.

"Welcome to Incredible News! I'm your trusty news reader John Journalist!" he said, looking directly at his teleprompter to the left of the camera. *"Joining me today is my partner Anne Anchorwoman! Yes, I will continue to shout my news to you until I develop throat problems because we all know that shouting makes news more legitimate! We have received a tip from one of our viewers that three terrorists working in a xenophobic terrorist cell have recently committed an act of terrorism in a small town that no one really cares about! Now back to you Anne. I said nothing worthy of discussion and I honestly could not give less of a shit, same as our bored viewers who are probably only watching because they have nothing else to do! What do you think about the situation?"*

"Well, John, I think this is terrible news, what with thousands of estimated deaths in a neighbourhood stretch of about fifty something people. This is hat-breaking, uh, I mean, of course, as well as heartbreaking," Anne said robotically, looking at the camera with an empty gaze and forced a smile. *"Now*

we'll initiate the countdown to the next newsfeed that will repeat the same information, but with five experts on terrorism that we have called in from around the globe going live in precisely three hundred and ninety-five seconds. The timer is shown in the bottom right of your television screen, and now, John will deliver an angry rant about how Santanic, uh, and as well as Satanic *word processors are now obviously radicalising young adults writing science-fiction conspiracy novels. Obviously, the war on Christmas and Satan has started already. Join the loop by listening to John Journalist's incoherent rant!"*

Albest cursed, and Jane shrugged indifferently. Finally, Jane said, "Well, we can deal. It's okay; it's not the worst thing that's happened thus far. I'll call Mr. Wang and figure something out. Where's the nearest toilet?"

Jane tried not to look panicked, while Albest took the opportunity to sneak off to buy a wide-brimmed hat from one of the travel stores close by. He tilted the fashion accessory to cover his face and carefully guided Jane to the toilet.

Within moments of them leaving, my phone vibrated, and I received a text on my phone. Flipping it open, the display revealed that Albest had sent the text.

Albest :> P3tr. Stay here. We'll
come back in 5min. Brb. A tall Asian
guy will give you a few things. Meet
later.
Peter:> Wtf. Why?
Albest:> 👆

I furrowed my eyebrows and plopped down
on one of the seats, cycling through my texts with
nervous energy for a period of time and button-
mashed the keyboard in anger as I tried to process
this piece of information. At this point, most of the
TV screens had been dominated by our pictures and
they weren't pretty. Like, seriously, they picked the
most unflattering photo of me possible.

An image of me drunk, unconscious, and battered
took up nearly a third of the screen. It was an office
party gone wrong; I'd drunk too much and gotten into
a fight. Albest had taken the photo as he had been
the only sober person at the party and I was blackout
drunk. The real magic was how he had managed to
sneak into a corporate party without anyone noticing
that he wasn't an employee. Somehow, that photo had
found itself onto the TV screen. A shameful moment
of my life, I suppose, and it was on view to the public

because I was now officially branded as a terrorist—and that might have been worse.

Time passed, and I think Anne Anchorwoman also concluded her short segment. I couldn't tell; it was like watching the weather report. My brain just wasn't doing a terribly great job of comprehending any of the information being presented.

About ten minutes later, a tall, non-descript Asian man with forgettable features walked past me, and tossed a package into my lap before walking off without so much as glancing in my direction.

I sent a reply text to Albest, as I nervously shoved the thing into my jacket, hoping no one saw the transaction.

Peter :> K. Got it.
Albest :> Meet us @ cubicle 7, gents.

I headed off towards the men's toilets, and counted the stalls from top to bottom. Knocking on the seventh cubicle, a voice rasped, "Occupied."

"It's me. Open the door," I said, annoyed. The voice belonged to Albest. He opened the door and I entered. Albest was sitting on the toilet with Jane. They quickly shuffled away from each other to make room for me as I entered. That was an awkward moment.

"Peter, it's time to show us the goodies," Albest said. A giant smile crept over his face as he saw the package that I was holding. The package was a brown, dog-eared, cardboard box about the size of a small book, and we quickly ripped it open to examine the contents.

"Ahh. Travel documents and Hollywood-style makeup kits. Oh, it's so convenient and thoughtful of them to give us these," Albest said with a weird tone. I can't tell whether he was just being sarcastic or whether he seriously meant it.

"What about the gun? How are we getting them through the customs?" I asked.

"We don't. Mr Wang is going to do that for us," Albest said, revealing a brown paper bag full of guns. The opening of the bag revealed an impeccably clean and shiny handgun with the name "Chekovs" embossed onto it with gold leafing. The side of the handle had an additional line of laser-engraved text, reading: YOU KNOW I'M GOING TO USE IT. OTHERWISE THIS GUN WOULDN'T EXIST. That was a damn good-looking gun. The elaborate design indicates that it probably wasn't a store-brand weapon, and more likely to be something that was custom-made down to the exact measurement of the gun barrel.

"I'm dropping this behind the bin," Albest stated. "And, if all goes to plan, he'll get someone to take care of it or something. I expect to have it back by the time we reach the Resistance."

After Albest said a tearful goodbye to his gun, we put on some makeup and a few other miscellaneous disguises to camouflage our identities, and had a quick look through our falsified travel documents before heading off to customs. Though Albest was forced to take his wide-brimmed hat off, we passed through and boarded the plane without incident. He was forced to give it up since there was no room in his backpack to contain it.

We maintained some idle talk after the plane took off and asked for a glass of water each from the hostess and avoided talking about the elephant in the room for a while.

After our plane landed and we arrived at our destination, we walked in silence, exhausted from the journey as we assumed a false identity to hide from the authorities. Airport security had been beefed up overnight with a significant influx of police patrolling and more than a few suit-wearing federal intelligence officers surveying the place.

Of course, after walking away from the airport in relief, I felt something was off. There was a mechanical hum, a buzzing whirr of machinery following not too far behind us. I snuck a few glances backwards, and saw a tall, Asian man wearing a helmet, a set of elbow pads and knee pads over an atrocious flannel shirt and jeans riding towards us on a Segway. That made him the *second* worst-dressed hipster that I'd seen that day.

Unsure of how I was supposed to react in a situation like this, I turned to my friends. "Um, there's an Asian metrosexual hipster wearing flannel shirt and jeans following behind us on a Segway. Should I be worried?"

"Normally, yes, but not right now," Jane said. "He's our contact. Wang Wu Er. I think he was the guy who handed you the package of travel documents and disguises. He's been following us since we entered the airport. How are you still surprised? Do you really think we would've gotten away with airport security this easily if it weren't for the fact that he was helping us?"

"Uh, good point. Should we stop and wait for him?"

"What? Wait for him?" Albest snorted in derision. "No, of course not. I hate that guy. He can follow behind on his Segway for all I care."

" . . . But do you know where you are going, though?" Jane interjected, sighing for what felt like the nth time in a row.

"No."

"Then why the hell are we walking in front of him?" Jane snapped. "We are going to get lost if we don't follow directions, you know? And also, have you forgotten about your fucking gun? The one that you keep going on and on about? He has it. Go get it back if you really want it."

Albest looked offended but, naturally, he decided not to comment and just obey Jane's "suggestion," waiting for Wu Er the weirdly-dressed Segway man to catch up to us.

"Oh, hey guys. Why didn't you wait for me?" His voice was a nasal whine. Funny, he had a voice that matched his face and personality perfectly.

"Mr. Wang," Albest said, attempting to craft an excuse. "We didn't see you behind us, and I'm sooo sorry. I was busy uh . . . working . . . on, um, talking about, uuuuh, politics! Yeah, we were busy talking about politics and that's why I didn't realise you were behind us."

I attempted to shuffle away from Albest, covering my face in embarrassment. Nobody wants about politics. Especially not now.

"Okay! No worries. I get it." His smile was a bit strained, but he stilled appeared upbeat, "Follow me. Jeremy will take us to the base."

"Also, can I have my gun back?" Albest asked bluntly, revealing himself to be a true master of diplomacy and tact, a brand of diplomacy that made Gunboat Diplomacy look subtle and sophisticated.

"Ah. Ah yes, of course you may have it. Here it is," Wang Wu Er said, his smile straining so hard that I thought he might pull a muscle in his face.

We followed him without much comment, partly because we couldn't think of what to talk about, but mostly because Jane was too busy glaring at Albest to really have the time to start small-talk and Albest was too busy looking like an asshole. I nodded, and walked forward, carrying the scene on my shoulders.

"So, Mister Wang, is it? My name's Peter, Peter Stewart, and yes, I introduce myself to everyone I meet. It's an odd compulsion."

"Oh you can call me Wu Er if you want," Wu Er said with a smile so damned radiant that it deserved its own toothpaste commercial. "How's your day?"

"Good so far. Haven't died yet. Ate my vitamins; chewed on airplane food; said my prayers and fucked off from my job. That's good, right?"

Wu Er chuckled. "Ah yes, I suppose that would

constitute as a good day. Listen, there's like, this guy who will be driving you guys into our secret base in this area with a really cool car. It's going to be amazing."

A slight sense of excitement welled up inside me, but what did you expect? It was the first time in my entire life that I had experienced an event so crazy that it felt like it was straight out of a thriller movie filled with A-list actors rather than something you would encounter in real life.

Even though I'd already been on the run for two entire days and had already experienced the gut-wrenching sadness of seeing my house and basically everything I owned disappear in a fiery ball of flames, it had never really given me that thrilling feeling of starring in my own spy film. Somehow, I felt like I was the insignificant extra that disappears from the bigger picture five minutes into act one. Nothing screams insignificance more effectively than having everything you own go up in flames and then finding out over national TV that you're also framed for the very event that ruined your life.

We arrived in a parking lot and waited for a while. We didn't wait long before a nondescript car slowly pulled into the parking lot and my heart leapt into my throat. I could not contain my excitement as the tinted windows rolled down, revealing a bald man peering out with a flat gaze. A chill travelled down my spine as I met his gaze and examined his face.

Something about his face bothered me. It felt . . . wrong. The man had all the features a normal face was supposed to have, but it also felt like the face was put together like jigsaw pieces from different sets. The face was eerie, like something straight out of the Uncanny Valley. It was too narrow, his eyes were too beady, his nose was too sharp, and his cheekbones looked like they'd been broken many times over. Combine that with a cleft chin, and you got yourself the Hannibal Lector look but with none of the charisma.

There was also something about his expression . . . or the lack thereof. It didn't feel natural. It gave the me impression that his face was paralysed. With a click, he unlocked the car doors.

He stared blankly at us (I don't think he was capable of being able to express any expression besides a default poker face) and gestured towards the open doors. "Jeremy. Get in."

Albest tensed up beside me, and Jane had slowly reached her hand into her handbag. Being the least prepared out of the three, I shuffled behind Albest and tried to remain as inconspicuous as possible.

We made a few polite grunts and nodded in response to his taciturn nature, and obediently got in the car. From the moment I met him, all of my survival instincts screamed at me that the man driving the car was dangerous. If this was a crime drama, then he would be suspect #1 for the murder of an innocent young woman that was brutally murdered and then mutilated, and the case would be closed within twenty minutes of the cops seeing his mug.

A smirked played at the edge of Jeremy's lips as he ignored Wu Er and started driving without giving so much as a warning. Wu Er rushed up and bashed his fists against the car window. A muffled cry of protest could be heard as he rushed up against the car.

Jeremy stopped the car and stared at Wu Er. His expression was obscured by the shadows dancing in the car. "What."

"Hey! What about me? Let me in! You can't expect me to ride my Segway all the bloody way back to HQ, now, can you? It's a long way there and I sure as hell ain't making that trip on my own. I wanna get in," Wu Er said indignantly, looking mildly offended.

"That's what I'm implying." Jeremy sneered at him, walking out of the car to stare down at him with an intimidating glare.

"Well, same to you too, you sad, sad little

cockroach." Wu Er spat out the sentence, as though it was the worst possible insult that he could muster. There's no way Jeremy would be offended by that, I thought, and observed the drama unfold outside with vague disinterest. "Playing the cool professional, eh? You're nothing beyond this petty façade that you've built; nothing but an empty, shallow being. Hey Jeremy, I saw your relative the other day, he was being sold for $34.99. What was he again? Oh yeah, a sack of pig flesh."

That set Jeremy off. With a roar, he yanked Wu Er off the Segway and slammed him into the body of another, albeit shittier, car nearby, setting off the alarm. Jeremy ignored it, grabbing Wu Er by the head again and slamming him into it again and again.

"YOU. TAKE. THAT. BACK." Jeremy was close to executing a brilliant fatality when he suddenly stopped a few centimetres away from Wu Er's face. His hands dropped to his side.

Wu Er smiled menacingly at him. Even though he seemed to be the weaker one in this situation, he looked triumphant. Through a mouthful of broken teeth, he spat out a glob of blood onto Jeremy's suit. "What are you going to do next, huh? *Pathetic.* You couldn't even reconcile with the fact that you have a shitty tattoo. What right do you have to insult me?"

Jeremy's face reddened to the colour of a tomato. If smoke came out of his ears, he would've completed his transformation into a pissed-off cartoon character. With a subconscious movement, he pulled on the collar of his shirt, tilting his head to the left, in an almost protective position. I spied an inky image on the side of his neck peeking out for a brief moment, before it was obscured.

A few seconds of silence passed by. He took out his car keys and opened the boot of the car. "Get in."

Wu Er froze. He looked back up. "Sorry?"

Jeremy pointed to the boot of the car again, and shoved Wu Er's Segway into it, before motioning towards Wu Er. "In."

Wu Er struggled to his feet as he, for a brief second, could not identify which direction he was facing. Wu Er limped towards the boot, and just as he was about to climb in himself, Jeremy kicked him inside and locked it. I stared in fright as Jeremy closed the car doors and started up the car again.

06

IT WAS A SURPRISINGLY SHORT RIDE FROM THE airport to the so-called secret location we were being taken to. Throughout the entire car ride, Jeremy made no attempts at starting a conversation. I didn't either, and didn't want to. The tense car ride felt way longer than it was.

Though no one said a word, instead of feeling bored, I was almost constantly at the edge of my seat, afraid of something happening. It's not an exaggeration to say that Jeremy radiated an aura of danger, and with what had just happened with Er Wu, there was no way I could feel safe in his presence. The entire process was kind of like making eye contact with a serial killer, I guess. On that happy note, when I actually got out of the car, I breathed a sigh of relief.

Someone dressed as a front desk employee came out of the building with a horrified expression. He didn't so much as glance at us, looking at Jeremy with a disgusted expression, before he turned to the boot of the car, where Wu Er was stashed along with his Segway. The man fiddled with the car a bit, before the boot popped open, revealing Wu Er. Battered and heavily injured, blood dribbled outwards from so many different places on his body that a small pool of blood had formed underneath him.

Shouting ensued as two people rushed out with a stretcher and flung Wu Er onto it. They rushed away quick enough, but a few more wearing Kevlar vests restrained Jeremy, and confiscated his car keys. It wasn't long before they started examining the car and the boot. The whole process lasted about three minutes as they processed everything with a frightening efficiency bordering, and they ignored us.

We were forced to sit there for a while, as Jeremy disappeared inside with three people surrounding him. Jeremy walked back out a few moments later, his face pale and blank. There was a wound on his neck, it was dark and burnt, as though something hard and hot was pressed against for an extended period of time. He looked at us. A few more seconds passed before he managed to squeeze out, "Follow me."

I would be lying if I said I wasn't scared, but we had nowhere else to go. We exited the car and followed Jeremy inside the building. As the adrenaline wore off, I finally had the sense to examine the place that I was taken to. It wasn't in the middle of the desert, nor was it a military base. It wasn't a lavish building, either, without any semblance of power or status, or anything that looked even remotely impressive.

Pop-culture generally placed top-secret organisations in suave places and I had admittedly been a huge fan of melodramatic buildings that made you feel important just by walking by it. There's a reason people enjoy visiting the Buckingham palace. But I was unfortunately disappointed by this ordinary-looking office building that looked positively *squashed* between the towering skyscrapers on the right and the shopping centre on the left.

The corners of my mouth twitched and I nervously followed Jeremy inside to meet with . . . whoever was going to meet me.

I think they overplayed the cloak-and-dagger thing a bit.

I was still quite curious as to what the hell just happened with Jeremy. He looked almost . . . afraid of something. The entire process had only taken about three minutes, but he walked out looking like he saw a ghost.

The whole 'tattoo' thing also felt a little out of left field. I didn't quite understand exactly why Wu Er felt so happy seeing his reactions. Surely a mere tattoo couldn't be *that bad*.

We passed through the lobby and arrived at a somewhat spacious room that had no real decorations besides tastefully dark wallpaper. A man was sitting in the room, typing away on a computer. He looked up from his computer and swept his gaze appraisingly over us.

The man was tall, skinny, and had sunken bloodshot eyes on a face that appeared to be 99% bone and 1% skin. In short, he looked like an anorexic skeleton with skin draped over it. He maintained eye contact for a while before he attempted to speak blandly, only to fail comically at that. "*Buona Sera.* I-I-I believe you have a lot of questions for me right now. Please, have a seat and let-let-let's have a slow chat."

"Alright, my name is Albest. Nice to meet you," Albest said politely, much to my surprise. Seeing Albest being composed and even-mannered while to talking to someone with a speech impediment was the most shocking thing that I had seen that night. "Can you please tell us— AHH! WHAT THE FUCK IS THAT!!"

We all collectively lost our shit as Jeremy's face literally *melted off* in front of us. And that was definitely not an exaggeration.

It started with his hair receding into his scalp, and then the disgusting sound of bones and meat crunching, before Jeremy's face changed into something so fucking atrocious that it made Voldemort's face look handsome; and I'm talking about Voldemort's face *after* it was fucked over with magic.

A grisly mess of pulpy flesh and misplaced bones appeared before us. I couldn't even identify the most basic facial features. To put it bluntly, Wade Wilson (or better known as Ryan Reynold's better half) would probably look more attractive than Jeremy at that moment.

As I steadied my breathing, I turned and stared enquiringly at the man who sat at the desk, still typing away on something without even the slightest change in his expression, as if this couldn't be more ordinary.

"Alright," I said. "What the hell just happened?"

The man sighed heavily, before speaking in a bored tone. "*Mi scusi, Signor Peter Stewart,* I thought something like this wouldn't surprise you, taking into consideration there are aliens from other planets here on Earth. I was wrong. Just think about it for a second. Do you really think there would be a civilisation out there advanced enough to travel through space and capable of discovering other planets with intelligent life on it—a feat that humanity hasn't managed to accomplish yet—and be unable to perform basic modifications on a-a human b-body? N-no. Their overall level of civilisation is already decades, if not centuries, ahead of our current level of technology. And Jeremy just happened to be a person that is the subject of an experiment on modifying facial structures to advance political espionage." He paused to type even more furiously on his computer before resuming his story. "Imagine ho-how horrifying the concept of a person who can alter their face at will is. They could get into basically any place they want and take whatever they want as well. Imagine if the president of an important country was replaced by someone else; an-and no one could tell the difference simply through comparing their physical traits. Keep in mind, Jeremy wasn't even a success."

"Sorry? He was a *failure*?" Jane said. I was personally not as surprised. I mean, his ability was far from perfect and, judging by the look of pain on his face, there was probably a limit to how long he could keep that going. There were probably more downsides to his ability as well, but I couldn't guess anymore with the little information I'd been given.

A look of curiosity flashed across Albest's face as he stared appraisingly at Jeremy. "So he can alter his entire facial structure, huh? Wouldn't his skull basically implode?"

The man finally stopped whatever he was doing and looked straight at us. "Good question. The answer is yes, but they managed to minimise the damage by performing lobotomy on him and literally making his brain smaller to prevent it from scraping against the bones while he changes his face. The downside is that speech and thinking in general become difficult. He's not an awfully talkative guy now. Ha. He's been with us ever since he was 'discarded.' And, *recently,* he mi-m-misbehaved. Don't worry. He'll be p-punished more. *Tutto bene.*"

Jeremy's face paled further, though it was . . . difficult to tell. He trembled slightly, before he was escorted out of the room by the guards.

Albest exchanged a look with Jane. It was obvious that they had rehearsed the questions that they were going to ask shortly after. Jane stepped forward and started asking a few more questions. "Alright, we are done with the talk, then. Will living spaces be provided for us? And what will we have to do? What is the aim of this organisation? Everything we know is very vague thus far, and I would like some more details."

He raised his eyebrows before quickly printing out a sheet of paper with an address and room number on it, then took out three room cards from one of his desk drawers. "We anticipated your arrival, so it's natural that we have provided some rooms here for you. As for what you are going to do as a part of the Resistance . . . well, I guess it will depend on what you *want* to do. We wouldn't want to waste a talented soldier on an . . . oh what's the word . . . office job! *Si!* Office job, f-for example."

He subtly motioned for us to leave the room with a very, very fake smile. The smile was disturbing, a row of jagged and blackened teeth. That didn't quite resemble a case of poor dental hygiene; perhaps more of a case of deterioration from the roots up.

Since we were smart people, we decided to leave the room without causing too much trouble. Something disturbed me about this place. The timetable in my hand told me that I'd be going on an orientation tour of the facilities with Albest and Jane first thing in the morning, with an assessment session in the afternoon—whatever that was.

Albest, Jane and I headed towards our assigned rooms under the watchful gazes of security cameras that swerved to follow our path with each step we took. I looked behind me as I closed the doors, and saw Albest staring at the cameras. Looking at it, unblinking.

I headed into my room. I needed to sleep. Good night. Sleep tight. To wake up in the morning light.

07

I OPENED MY EYES AS A BUCKETFUL OF ICE WATER drenched my face. The shrill sound of an alarm clock clambered nearby. That infernal device sounded like it was stuck somewhere in-between an opera where the fat lady was hitting the high note and a robot fucking a dumpster. I closed my eyes again and threw the damned abomination to the side of the room.

Groaning, I got up from my bed feeling like shit. The ringing did not subside. I still felt like a dozen construction workers were inside my head, hitting it with sledgehammers. Goddamit, did they build that fucking thing out of steel or some shit? Why isn't it broken yet?

"WAKE UP! TRAINEE!"

I looked at the buff, steroid-pumped, manly-man standing in front me, and returned my gaze to the empty beer cans beside my bed. I was experiencing a hangover, and the man who woke me was having none of it.

Last night, I vaguely remembered Albest, being the kind of person who could not give less of a shit about having anything that resembles a schedule, had woken me up in the middle of the night (again), and dragged Jane and I into a liquor shop to buy a case of beer. What happened next was a shitload of drinking and, now, a nasty headache. Don't play drinking games, kids; it is a very good way of getting dangerously wasted.

I went through my morning routine and told the asshole to wait outside. Wait, how did he get the keys to my room? I thought it was private. He told me to go to the front lobby when I was ready, and then they'll tell me what to do. He gave me three minutes, and he made sure that I knew that the consequences of not being able to complete his demand weren't pretty.

Albest and Jane ambled out of their rooms, presumably having endured the same unceremonious awakening as myself. I felt much better about how my day was going. The birds were chirping, and the sun felt like it was shining brighter. Subconsciously, I even started humming sunshine and lollipops as I heard Albest and Jane moan and groan like zombies.

"Man, last night was crazy. We're never doing that again," Jane said. Her glare towards us intensified even more, if that was possible.

Albest looked sheepish. "Hey, we had a good time drinking and partying, that's that. Also, I never knew you liked rock and roll. Huh."

"Well, just because I'm a librarian and have a degree in IT doesn't mean I'm a bookish person with no taste in music, Albest," Jane retorted, rolling her eyes.

There were only two cameras in the hallway, occupying the adjacent left and right edges of it. I noticed them slowly tilting themselves to follow us. On every floor, there was a tacky poster of a man with three eyes standing tall and content with his hands clasped in front of his chest piously, with the bottom line being 'TO AWAKEN TO THE TRUTH IS OUR SACRED AND DIVINE DUTY. SWALLOW THE PILL AND BECOME AS GODS.'

Okay, there was some tacky posters here and there, but nothing worthy of note.

We trailed behind the muscle-builder down to the lobby. The lobby was a wonderful place. It had a jar full of peppermint candy, air conditioning, and vigilant cameras on every side of the room. Really, the lobby felt . . . familiar to me. Walking around it gave me a lucid sense of déjà vu—similar to the office building I spent the better part of my life working at, but more in focus, I suppose. Everyone there seemed to be there for a purpose, as uniform-wearing men with military-esque helmets marched out the door in single-file and men in fancy suits holding fat briefcases entered in a near-constant stream. It was like watching a fine-tuned machine.

The sofas were comfy, elaborately designed, and looked more valuable than my car. Well, before it burnt to ashes along with my house, that is. Albest wiggled in his seat for a bit, and started practising the mysterious art of eyebrow wiggling.

To this day, I still haven't figured out how to wiggle my eyebrows, yet my friend could do it with near-effortless ease. I'm jealous, if I'm honest with myself.

Jane tapped away on her phone, fixated on something suitably distracting since there was no one in the lobby who bothered to greet us, and we didn't want to interact with the drill-sergeant stereotype.

I briefly considered whether I should go over and have a look at what was so interesting on her phone, but then thought better of it. I have standards, and wasting time invading someone else's privacy just to check whether they're looking at cat videos or not was clearly below mine.

The distant sound of shoes echoing through the vast lobby soon reached my ears, and I turned in response to greet the owner of said shoes.

He was the man who greeted us. He was wearing an expensive bespoke suit with matching leather shoes that must have taken a lot of effort to get into. His tie bore the most immaculate knot I had ever seen. It was the kind of gentlemanly knot that would make any man feel shame at their inadequate amount of knowledge of tie-tying knots. On the top of his breast pocket was a nametag that read: WARREN, ADMINISTRATOR.

"*Buon giorno*, I-I assume you have already guessed what topics we'll be discussing today," Warren stuttered. "I am your superior and I'll b-be giving you a brief tour of our facilities. T-the man over there, yeah, will be your coach. He'll be in charge of your training. Meet Steve." He smiled, revealing his sickening smile again, as he patted Steve on the back.

"Where's Jeremy?" I asked. "The guy who was with us last night?"

His smile disappeared, a chill crept down my spine, and I felt cold sweat travel down my forehead as his smile faded away. There was almost something creepy about how quickly emotion fled from his face. "He is currently . . . away. Would you like to see him?"

"Nah. No thank you. We have better things to do," Albest said. I was relieved. Myself, I wasn't sure whether I could've opened my mouth in that moment. Unlike me, Albest was completely unaffected by the man's intimidating presence.

The man stared long and hard at Albest, who demonstrated a unique ability to display all the fucks he didn't give by sipping water and pretending to read a magazine.

"V-very well. Back to the topic at hand. Steve wi-will train you and make sure you don't die or piss yourself from fright every time you see something new. For the next two months or so, he'll be giving you basic training to improve your general physical ability. I-it is mandatory. Even if y-you get assigned to an office job, you must d-demonstrate the ability to defend yourself from armed assailants in different scenarios."

"A-a-almost every recruit that comes through here will ask basic questions like 'where was the training taking place?', 'will it take a lot of effort?', and such questions. So, I'm here to make sure you get answers to these questions and feel happy. Please do not worry, the two-month program is tailored towards average adults who have no experience in the military or handling weaponry. Furthermore, the program will be adjusted based on a case-by-case basis. We will never ask a person who needs twenty seconds to finish a hundred-meter dash to finish it in five."

We nodded, it was pretty straight-forward. The idea that we would be trained by a hardened muscle pig with no finesse or care was a movie cliché done to death and, therefore, it was easier to accept.

"N-now, we'll be giving you a brief tour of our facilities. I-in t-the afternoon, you will start training with Steve," Warren said, handing us freshly-printed handouts of our schedule for the day. "Follow me."

With an electric whirr, the doors slid open. The sweltering summer air rushed into the air-conditioned room as we stepped out into the streets and headed off.

Our destination was a good walk from our nice little office-building/hotel. The path wound into the deepest parts of the city. There was a conspicuous lack of urban noise, city-pollution and thoughtless littering here. No crumpled cans of soda, no aged posters or mottled pieces of cardboard on the sidewalk. The further we walked, the quieter the surroundings became. Until, at one point, there was no background ambience at all. It was completely devoid of the familiar roars of the car engine, the pedestrian noise, and the irregular flickering sounds of fluorescent lights from nearby stores. There was Resistance men on almost every corner, though, non of them was holding a gun, and every one of them have some sort of pseudo-militaristic insignia on the collar.

An austere building appeared in front of us. Concrete on all sides, hardened cement slabs for ground with a tall, indomitable fence surrounding it. There were no key holes or pin pads. Instead, Warren withdrew out a strange, credit-card like object and waved it across a section of the wall that looked just like any other section of the wall, and the door slid open.

Walking in, I spied a dozen cameras either perched on the fences, or on the corners of the building. Several patrolling security guards were wearing something resembling body cams. The distinct clicking sound of my feet meeting hard wood surprised me. Much of the interior of the building seemed to have a wooden look and feel to it, with warm lighting filtered through beautiful muti-coloured windows and what appears to be renaissance-style murals. A complete antithesis to the cold modernistic exterior design, the building seemed to have been designed by two separate architects with distinctly different styles, and at least one violent disagreement on creative directions, with how sharp the contrast between the exterior and the interior was.

"Ah, t-the pride of Cell PX-300456," Warren said, a hint of pride tinged in his voice. "The Re-resistance i-is composed of separate cells working w-worldwide. We are cell unit PX-300456. R-remember that."

"So, uh, Warren, can I ask you a question?" Jane held her hand up timidly. "What, exactly, do you do around here?"

Warren froze. He stopped mid-walk, and I almost collapsed into him.

"Heh. Heh. Hehhehheh. U-uh, I-I-I m-m-manage resources for a multinational secret o-o-organisation, a-am in regular contact with diplomats, and . . . uh, manage insurance claims. Yep. AlsoonweekendsIvolu nteeratanonprofitcampforsociallystigmatisedyoutha ndadults." Warren laughed very loudly and nervously for a few moments before he hurriedly stuttered through something that sounded like an indirect confession of guilt.

"Sorry what? I didn't catch the last part." Jane blinked. None of us caught the last part. Did . . . did he say something? Something about a non-profit weekend camp, I think.

"N-never mind. I-it is not important anyways," Warren said as he picked up the pace again and continued walking.

One hallway crashed into another, forming endlessly large and complicated mazes of labyrinthian depth, to my annoyance. My legs were growing tired.

After what felt like a century of endless walking, we entered a well-lit room with poorly-assembled filing cabinets, chairs with uneven legs and nails poking out, and tables with large scratches decorating the sides. The poor craftsmanship involved here reminded me of the first time that I bought DIY furniture—similar results.

There was a person pacing around the room, with a plastic cast covering the better part of his upper body. That person was Wu Er. He stopped pacing when he noticed us, eyes lighting up as he strode towards us.

"Oh hello there! Are you here for the orientation tour?" he said, giggling. "I'm the guy in charge of the facility here. There's not much for me to do around here while injured. Might as well as give you a tour of the place, eh?"

Warren went to one of the larger tables and started

brewing coffee for himself with a packet of instant coffee and some hot water. Seeing the abundance of instant coffee packets, I brewed a cup of coffee for myself. Wu Er insisted that we wear plastic shoe covers and coveralls as we entered an airlock and was sprayed down with some sort of cleaning fluid. We continued our tour of the place.

"These are the testing areas," he said. "While we are admittedly not much of a science facility, there is no need to worry about hygiene or sanitary infections here, the entire laboratory is an ISO-3 Clean Room in compliance with ISO 14644-1 up to the latest revised guidelines with a smart laminar-flow air circulation system that goes through 2 cycles per every sixty seconds and state-of-the-art Hazmat containment procedures in place and several foam-sprays installed throughout the facility during emergencies. Every once in a while, we need to test out the safety mechanisms and fail-safes in place for our weapons and other items in our inventory. Every cell in the Resistance receives supplies from a mysterious cabal of people called Cell A. Never saw head or tail of 'em, but every other month, boxes of supplies turn up. Like, no security camera footage or anything, and they always appear along with a dossier of monthly assignments." He briefly demonstrated the usage of a few clunky-looking devices that looked like shotguns with sawn-off barrels. "And it is up to us, the good men and women working here to engineer the gadgets and gizmos our field agents use and to reverse-engineer any alien-tech found on the field. Hazardous contaminants can easily spread in an unsafe environment, which is why anyone working here will be formally required to undertake some coursework on proper PPE procedures regardless of whether or not they're in a technical position. There are certain risks involved in handling dangerous materials, and that is why there are checklists of proper PPE procedures to study for every worker here."

The weapons were . . . disappointing. None of them looked futuristic and the majority of the armoury seemed to be populated by bullets for conventional guns rather than, oh I don't know, lightsabres and plasma cannons. The most advanced piece of technology in the armoury was what appeared to be some sort of Roomba-transformer.

It was kind of like Michael Bay's CGI-trocity given life. Yeah, imagine that, but a Roomba. One minute, it was cleaning the floor, the next minute, it transformed into a . . . well, I don't actually know what it was, but it looked like the unholy lovechild of every single firearm on Earth and a dog. Albest picked it up and started violating it with a creepy stare in his eye. He stared at it with the intensity of a pervert eyeing a supermodel.

"Ah! I see you've taken an interest in our Household Intelligent Cleaning and Klaxon-sounding Laser-guided Electrical Rover! Do you want me to deliver a convenient and long-winded exposition of the backstory behind its conception and how it was, ultimately, built for greatness as it purges our floor of unclean filth of both the literal and figurative kind?"

"Nah, we're good. The acronym stencilled onto its back . . . " Albest said uncertainly. "Um, I'm not quite sure that HICKLER was a good acronym. HICKLER sounds like a teen slang used to describe racist country musicians."

"Oh, yeah. About that . . . Warren was the supervisor for the entire development of this project so, naturally, he got the right to name it. Rumour has it that Warren had an entire secret basement R&D facility built just to test out ol'HICKLER over there. Crazy what kinda tales bored researchers will make up about the boss, huh?"

Albest looked impressed while I feigned disinterest out of fear of looking like an idiot.

"That's one convenient piece of technology you've

got there," Albest said as a grin travelled up his face. I knew that shit-eating grin anywhere. It was the one he got whenever a bad idea popped into his head, like mailing a bag of dildos to his friend, for example.

"Say, why did Jeremy get offended at you last night?" I hurriedly changed the topic. Anything to get Albest's mind off whatever the hell he was thinking about.

"Well, the field agents found Jeremy during a raid," Warren said. "He was naked and tossed into a dark, sunless cell to be left to rot. It was an experimentation facility, as you know." He started laughing, wheezy short bursts of it as he told the story. "He's got two Chinese characters tattooed on the back of his neck. At first, we thought it was his name or some sort of identifier, but ahahaha, oh god, just take a look at it."

He flipped open his cell phone and opened up a picture. The picture showed the back of a man's neck, with an artsy tattoo printed onto it. I squinted at the picture, and it took me a few moments to remember my high school LOTE Chinese classes. But as soon as I recognised them, I started laughing. The two characters were:

蟑螂

Well, so much for eloquence. Jane and Albest looked at me in confusion for a few moments before

I explained the joke to them. "Ahahaha ... Well, the tattoo essentially means cockroach in Chinese. Was that just a bad tattoo?"

Wu Er nodded. "Oh yeah. So, after some time, around the time he was kidnapped to become a test subject, we found out that he'd been tattooed with the symbol. The end result was, well, not pretty. We laughed about it behind his back for a few weeks. I think he's still pretty hung up about it. Called us insecure nerds while he was at it, too."

"Alright. Now, allow me to give you a comprehensive tour of our filing offices, the classified document archives, and secret document incineration procedures to complete the orientation. After all, we're short on personnel there, so there's a chance that you'll get to work there. I think."

Albest remained attentive the entire time. Which was almost always a bad sign. He occasionally made notes of what Wu Er would talk about and record it on his phone.

After giving us the extensive tour around and showing us where the security cameras were, Wu Er told us, with a long-winded expository dialogue, all about the specific actions and types of security breaches that could trigger the alarm sirens and automated security systems.

Jane then had a deep and in-depth conversation with him about the filing system the Resistance uses to organise the case file. He was quickly defeated in terms of data management as he attempted to explain how 'advanced' and 'complex' their filing systems were to the librarian who had seen the Dewy Decimal System. To my knowledge, I vaguely remember at least five encyclopedia's worth Dewy Classifications stashed behind the librarian's desk and I'm pretty sure something is terribly wrong if the Resistance somehow has a system more complex than the ones used by libraries all over the world to keep track of their catalogues.

Defeated, Wu Er continued his presentation of the facility, "Our entire facility here is so secret and secure that it is physically impossible to rob us blind with how impenetrable our security systems are. Cameras installed at every corner—except the drinking fountains and the toilet areas and the coffee break areas; the carefully scheduled security shifts that last more than five hours; and the entrance that will only open to anyone with the proper identification card . . . *just try to rob us.*"

Wu Er managed to sounded enthusiastic again as he finished his sentence. Hopefully, Albest wouldn't take that as a challenge. He led us through every nook and cranny like a single parent flaunting their kid's perfect exam scores. "In fact, we are so secure and up-to-date with our defence systems that even our emergency exits are protected by an eighteen-digit alphanumeric combination code that changes randomly every month."

"Wait, you're saying that the emergency exits are password protected." Jane turned around. She had looked unimpressed at first, but now a look of panic shrouded her face.

"Precisely!" Wu Er nodded.

"So you're saying that, in the event of an emergency, you would need to enter a passcode in order to get the thing to unlock," Jane said slowly, looking at Wu Er as though he was a madman. *Mad Men*, a great TV show; more people should watch it. My mum liked it.

"Of course. We wouldn't want some alien spy sneaking away with our top-secret documents, now, would we? Besides, in the event of an emergency—which has never happened thus far, and it never will because of how secure and safe this location is—you can count on the trusty Keeper of Passwords in the security department to give you the password. As he is responsible for remembering the passwords every month. He's got an amazing memory! You should see him recount the number of pi up to the twenty-seventh digit."

It took a while for it to sink in that the Keeper of Passwords was an actual job belonging to a very real human being, not a computer program. And on that happy note, we concluded our orientation of the secret research facility/office/archive/warehouse of Cell PX-300456.

We had a brief and uninteresting lunch break, which, at Jane's insistence, was taken outside the building and at a shitty Mexican food restaurant nearby. Something about "tempting fate by staying in that death trap." You know, the ordinary stuff.

Twenty minutes later, Steve showed up, looking at us with a scowl on his face and a sour attitude.

"WELL!!?? ARE YOU FINISHED WITH YER BLOODY LUNCH YET?" he roared, looking at us with an intimidating glare as he took a bite from his apple and pointed his threatening finger at us.

"Aren't you doing the same thing as us? I mean, you're still eating food," Albest said, looking entirely too relaxed and nonchalant than was socially acceptable at this moment. I assure you that I looked properly frightened, like a deer in the spotlight.

"THAT'S NOT THE POINT!" Steve yelled. "NOW, I'M GOING TO GRAB A 'GOTTLE OF

GUINNESS AND YOU BETTER BE FINISHED SHOVING FOOD DOWN YER PIEHOLES BY THE TIME I GET BACK, MATE, OR Y'ALL GUNNA BE SORRY."

With that, Steve stormed off.

We wolfed down our lunch. Felting anxious, I started tapping my feet as I waited for our screamer-in-chief to return.

He tossed an empty bottle of beer down onto ground, and started chugging down his second can. After a loud burp, he stared at us. "Now, my name is . . . uuuhhhh, Steve Murkle."

We introduced ourselves, and followed him down through the lobby, past the elevators, and down a left turn to stand in front of a door marked "Broom Closet."

Steve pressed his greasy palm onto the door, the door swung open, and I realised that the broom closet was a lie. It was not broom closet.

As the door swung open, I saw a descending spiral staircase leading underground. Oh boy, the staircase was made of those fancy anti-slip fibre glass materials. It looked fancy, and very expensive.

I walked down the staircase and came to find a gym underneath the building. Okay, it wasn't the most shocking thing I'd seen all day, nor was it the most surprising. I nodded at the gym, feeling somewhat impressed.

There was no high-tech training equipment lying about or any fancy architectural designs that indicated that this place was any different from a normal gym except for the fact it was underground and, somehow, that made it all worth it. I mean, *of course we can't use the gym that was* literally *down the block*. But nooooo, since it was the Resistance, apparently everything must be placed under a secretive veil of cloak-and-dagger.

The entire underground gym was filled with the same old shitty two-hundred-dollar treadmills and department-store dumbbells that every other gym had. Kind of disappointing, really.

Steve shoved us onto the treadmills, connected breathing and heart-rate measuring apparatuses onto us and then started shouting again. "ALRIGHT YE MUCKLED DARNED MAGGOTS. WE'LL MEASURE YOUR AEROBIC CAPACITY FIRST AND ANAEROBIC CAPACITY BEFORE MOVING ONWARDS TO DETERMINING AN EXERCISE REGIMEN THAT SUITS YOUR BODY TYPE. YER GONNA STAY 'TILL DINNERTIME, SO GET A MOVE ON! WEAPONS TRAINING IN ONE HOUR! NOW GET RUNNNING!"

We started running, and within five minutes, I was already at the brink of collapsing into an exhausted heap. Jane didn't fare much better.

Ignoring the oddball known as Albest, who had taken free running courses and self-defence classes before, Jane was a librarian and I don't know about you, but working in the library seven days a week doesn't seem like a recipe for physical fitness to me. As for me, I was just a helpless bystander who'd been dragged into a hot mess grâce à my friend Albest, so I'll be honest here, I didn't take free running courses and I didn't attend self-defence courses as a hobby. In fact, as an office worker, I have to say, I'm not exactly in tip-top shape.

After what felt like an eternity, we finally moved onto weapons training. Really, it was not much of an improvement. Steve aimed a gigantic paintball gun at us, threatening to open fire every time we made a mistake. Not an improvement. With no breaks or any opportunity to rest, we learnt how to use knives and guns the hard way. If it wasn't for the fact that the guns were loaded with practise rounds and the fact that the knives were ceramic imitations, we would have been dead by the end of the practise session.

It went on for a long, miserable time before Steve reluctantly called, "STOP!" as Jeremy carried a bucket of food into the room. After the training ended, we were famished. With the bucketful of questionably healthy fast food placed in front of us, Albest and I tore apart the chicken wings of victory and stuffed our mouths with food while Jane devoured the Coleslaw salad.

Jeremy pointed to me, then nodded. I looked at him with a confused expression. Was he asking me to come with him? He moved up the staircase, and I followed him away. I looked behind me, and saw Albest stacking my uneaten chicken wings onto his plate. Fucking Albest.

Muttering curses, I followed Jeremy into the elevator. He pressed a button, the doors swung shut, and we began to ascend. I endured the journey in silence. Jeremy wasn't much of a talker and I couldn't give enough of a shit to try and strike up a conversation.

The elevator doors slid open, and I walked out with Jeremy, surveying the surroundings. Cameras swept the office floor as I walked around. Bland, white fluorescent lights hummed and flickered on the ceiling, illuminating the general area.

Office workers milled aimlessly to-and-fro from their desks, pressing buttons and taking calls and wandering towards other areas of the floor carrying multiple pieces of paper in their hands. My heart sank.

"You will start work here from tomorrow onwards," Jeremy said, as he affixed a soulless stare at me.

He guided me to a desk squished inside a tiny cubicle, devoid of any personality or design. A blue swerve chair was under the desk. It wasn't a bad chair. It looked comfortable enough.

There was no stationery on the desk. There was, however, a generic desktop computer and a headset attached to said computer. It was almost as if I had never left my old job at all. An unenergetic young man handed me a list of things to memorise and a small notepad already covered with scribbles before heading off to grab another cup of coffee from the coffee machine nearby. There was a comically large amount of coffee powder stacked besides it. It was almost as if they fear that there needs to be emergency backups of emergency-backup-coffee-powders in case the coffee machine ran out.

Jeremy tried his best to give me a comprehensive tour in silence and introduced me to my new job, which would start tomorrow as part of the orientation program.

It was pretty much a call centre job, and I was

supposed to be taking calls in the call centre (yeah, it was pretty surprising that they had one. It never occurred to me that the Resistance would have a call centre to deal with problems, but I guess it kind of made a lot of sense that they would). In other words, there was nothing particularly exciting there. Every single phone call I received would contain sensitive information and my only task was to push buttons and forward the calls to people who had the relevant clearance to deal with the hypothetical problems. This basically killed every single conversation before it started and drained the fun out of things.

The tour pretty much wrapped itself up at that point. I walked back, bought a sandwich from the canteen, and collapsed into an exhausted heap on the luxurious sofa in the lobby after the damned-near-torture amount of information that I was forced to process on the first goddamned day of orientation. Yes, I was disgustingly average, and I spent the entire day discovering just how shitty my capabilities were.

"Goddammit, why did they even bother telling us that they wouldn't overdo the exercises for?" I complained. "Even the 'warmups' were fucking terrifyingly exhausting! I feel like my entire body is about to fall apart."

Albest shrugged nonchalantly. "Well, to be honest, it *was* pretty simple and straightforward. The warmup was essentially just asking you to log five kilometres on the treadmill at jogging speed. It was not that hard compared to me being forced to run thirty kilometres." He sighed, "So, where'd they take you? We were in the middle of eating dinner and you just . . . kinda left."

"Right, so you know, apparently, there's a call centre in the building. And starting from tomorrow, I'm going to be working there," I said, releasing a grunt of frustration. "It's just like my old job. It was . . . frustrating, but at the same time, I feel relieved. I know what to do and I don't feel like I'm being pushed out of my comfort zone. That's good, right?"

"Well, I don't know about that," Albest said curtly, looking uncertain of what he could add to the conversation.

"So, do you wanna go on a shopping trip tonight? I could use some spare clothing, and hey, maybe you could spend some time with Jane," I suggested. I mean, I did suppose I could go on a shopping trip or two. I didn't have any personal belongings at this point, and buying an alarm clock and a few other living essentials could be a good idea.

Albest coughed shyly as he averted eye contact. Albest had a habit of disguising his embarrassment or nervousness behind coughing or covering his face, as if somehow that would make him look more in-control. "Well, speaking of which, there's a night market nearby. I heard it was a wonderful place to buy souvenirs and clothing."

I shrugged. It was rare to see Albest acting flustered and not like a knob. Besides, it was not like I had anything on my schedule for the night. Who knew, maybe something exciting would happen during our trip. I didn't know enough about Jane to conclude whether they were a good match or not, but sometimes love can work even when the two people in question have nothing in common.

"So, you going to ask Jane to come with us while I wait here, or do you want me to go up with you?" I raised a quizzical eyebrow.

"I think I can manage to do that alone," Albest assured me hurriedly, as he leapt up from his seat and sprinted for the elevator.

About fifteen minutes later, he bounded down the stairs trying to contain his excitement. He was rubbing his hands together in that cheesy manner that all clichéd evil maniacs seemed to do whenever they were hatching an evil scheme. "Come on, Jane said she'll meet us at eight in front of *that* coffee shop. You know which one I'm talking about."

He was right, I did know which coffee shop he was talking about. It would be impossible to *ever* forget that coffee shop. While Warren guided us to the gym, we were at the back talking about some of the interesting local businesses around the place and he ended up becoming an unofficial tour guide. It was then we found . . . that.

It was an atrocious monstrosity. To me, it was, and always would be, *That* Coffee Shop. I shall never mention it under any other name. In my eyes *That* Coffee Shop eclipsed and predominated the whole entirety of the craft. You see, *That* Coffee Shop had the . . . unique, insightful architecture that made no goddamn sense. The architect who designed the building must have been the drug-intoxicated relative of Dr. Seuss. No other explanation could have explained why there was a *fucking circus of animatronics riding clown cars into and out of pre-built tunnels and railroad tracks on the building whilst waving their mechanical arms around like it was the end of the world*. But no, apparently the designers decided that petty things such as "budgets", "building codes", and "reality" weren't factors worthy of being considered during the construction of the building.

As the largest and most offensively extravagant coffee shop around, there was really no other choice except to go there to drink coffee.

The worst thing about the swirly mess of geometrical shapes that I deign to call a building was that it required a university degree to be properly confused about it. Those who saw the fractal images and the Fibonacci sequence incorporated into the interior designs would probably just see it as that, but I saw it as a call for help from lonely scientists, mathematicians, and underpaid Arts majors who couldn't find meaningful jobs. I assume English Majors are happy with their degree, as with the Gender Studies Majors.

With polite interest, I marched with Albest towards the café in the urban districts, waiting for Jane while arguing about the difference between graffiti and street art as we walked past a suitably unimaginative set of names painted on the wall with a love heart beside it in bright neon-green spray paint (as if it wasn't bad enough already). But Albest decided to argue that, because art was subjective, a simple scribble on the wall could also be considered art depending on the value it offered to the viewer . . . and so we argued about the further intricacies of art and how vandalism was different from that. Before we knew it, we were at the café entrance.

Typing in one angry Google search after the other, Albest furrowed his eyebrows in confusion. "That's strange. The signal here is funny. The lag shouldn't take this long, and . . . hold on a minute, why are my phone settings set to public?"

"Um," I said nervously. "That doesn't sound good. Is something wrong?"

He was about to say yes before Jane walked into view and, of course, he immediately snapped his phone shut and took out the batteries. "Nope. Absolutely nothing is wrong. Let's go on a shopping trip! Nothing will get in my way of enjoying my shopping trip."

Albest laughed. He didn't sound relaxed; he sounded like he had already taken three shots of black coffee and we hadn't even entered the café yet.

Jane had really put some effort into picking out the clothes she was wearing. She wore a flannel jacket over a striped shirt, and coupled that with light-coloured shorts that looked really good on her. Jane looked stunning in a way that I thought only people with entire teams of professional and passionate make-up artists could manage. She wore a smile as she tilted her head in curiosity. "What were you guys talking about? I could hear it all the way from here."

Albest sheepishly replied, "It was nothing much. Just a polite discussion of our refined views about politics, abstract modern art and how its many forms are generally recognised but not accepted within the wide community of art appreciators."

Well that certainly sounded impressive, but it was ultimately nothing more than fluff and blather used to disguise his ignorance of fine arts and to make him look more educated.

Jane chuckled. "Well, I thought I heard more than a few swear words in there as well. I wouldn't think appreciating art had much to do with other people's intelligence or outward appearances. Just because Peter used too much hair gel this morning doesn't mean you should laugh about it."

Albest looked appropriately sheepish and embarrassed as he realised that some of the slightly more . . . personal aspects of our discussion may or may not have been overheard by someone else. I snickered, thoroughly enjoying the mortified expression on his face before realising that I had been indirectly insulted as well.

"Hey, what did you mean by that? My hair is just, you know, *naturally like thick and oily*. I don't, like, even use hair gel that much, you know?" I choked. Seriously though, I never used chemical products in my hair (well, half the time it was because I couldn't afford it. Most of the expensive brands cost fifty dollars per bottle. The cheaper brands offered a slick product line of slightly-wet cement collected from a nearby construction site. The local pharmacy near the place where I once lived was owned by a sadist who enjoyed the look of pain and despair on his customers' faces as they were forced to choose between the ridiculously overpriced hair products by good brands and the ridiculously overpriced hair products by brands that were still struggling to recover from lawsuits that claims that their products are causing hair-loss within their users and the cheap hair products that were essentially an au naturel recipe of cement mixed with animal poop).

I ended up arguing with Jane and Albest half-jokingly about meaningless things as we walked around some of the more interesting stores nearby that sold creative trinkets designed with the sole intent of scamming money out of the hands of the poor tourists.

Roughly ten minutes into the walk, Jane took out her phone, which had been vibrating nonstop for a while. She dropped her happy demeanour as she typed back a quick text. "Um, hey, this might sound like it came out of nowhere . . . but I think we're being followed. I just received a few weird text messages. Come on, let's go."

"Walk over to that large clothing shop and observe from there," Albest said. "We might be able to identify whoever our stalker is and there's even the possibility of losing our tail in the crowd." He smiled as he observed the crowd. "It's not like this is the first time we've been tailed. Happens more frequently than you'd think when your name gets placed onto the shit list of powerful groups."

"What should we do?" I whispered. The aliens had the technology to give damned superpowers to ordinary joes, and the only thing worse than being chased by a crazy murderous assassin was being chased by a crazy murderous assassin *with superpowers*. I felt like I was stuck in a childish game of one-upmanship on how ridiculous things could get.

Albest shrugged. "We'll figure it out along the way."

We entered the clothing store and pretended to actually give a shit about menswear. Albest and Jane discreetly conversed about what we should do next. "Look, if we spend too long in the clothing store, it might give away the fact that we already know that we're being followed," Albest said. "The best course of action is to try and lure our friend into a place that's strategically advantageous for us and less crowded. Peter, do you still have that crumpled information brochure with you? I might need to have a look at it again right now since I haven't exactly gotten too familiar with the area yet."

"Wait, gimme a sec," I said, furrowing my brows in tight concentration as I checked my pockets for the crumpled pamphlet that Albest gave me before we got on the plane. I'd almost forgotten I had it. Seriously, when was the last time you paid careful attention to an information pamphlet?

I fumbled through my pockets for it, then the rest of my clothing, and eventually yanked the crinkled thing out of my back pocket. I gave an embarrassed grin towards Albest and Jane, handing them the tourists' brochure.

Albest examined the map with a serious expression on his face. He casually took us on a leisurely stroll towards a side entrance, exiting into another stall, then pressing deeper and deeper into the labyrinthian night market.

After becoming sufficiently lost within the city and after making sure our tails were at least seven stalls away from us, he took out a pen and circled our position. "This is roughly where we are. It's possible for us to reach anywhere within the circle I've drawn in five to ten minutes of speed-walking. I think we can try and take down our tail. What do you think?"

"What are our odds?" Jane asked, keeping an eye on the tail.

"Pretty good. Now we outnumber them, and we can *kick ass.*" A grin spread from the corner of Albest's mouth as he scribbled a few indecipherable notes onto the map. "There are three places on the map that give us a territorial advantage against our unknown tail over there."

With that, he violently jabbed at the three places on the map. "One of our choices is a dark alleyway that's right next to a major intersection, so it could give us an escape route if things don't go as planned. The other option is to go to the back of this supermarket. It will be more spacious there, and there probably won't be any people running about near the back of a supermarket at this time of day. This place will also give us the upper hand as we might find some weapons lying about. We could, of course, also face off against him near the police station, and then dump his unconscious ass there once we are done and Spiderman our way of there. Don't worry, I don't think there are any security cameras there."

With practised ease, he gave the crinkled map back to me and waited for us to say something. We assessed our options for a short while before quickly coming to a unanimous decision of taking the route to the back of the supermarket. I figured no one really wanted to be stuck inside a dark alleyway fending off dangerous individuals *or* try their luck to see whether or not they were going to get arrested right outside a police station for attempted murder.

With Albest and Jane in the lead and me hiding behind them, we made our way forward.

Simply walking into open space with no one around might alert the guy to the fact that something was up and make him become more cautious, which would be bad. So, we tried our best to look like we were still aimlessly wandering around, and I made a scripted mime of needing to go to the toilet, splitting off from Albest and Jane to backstab our stalker if we got the chance.

As Albest and Jane neared the back of the supermarket, our tail behind them made his move. Stepping out of the shadows, right into our trap . . .

Instead, two men dressed in black and wearing cheap dollar store masks ran towards us. We didn't have the number advantage, and from the looks of it, they knew what they were doing. Fuck.

"Wait, there are *two* people following us?" Albest shouted in shock, loud enough for me to hear it all the way out at the back, behind the trash cans—which, for your information, smelled absolutely atrocious, like a can of expired tuna marinating in a slushy pile of rotten fruits and honey on a sweltering summer night. But given where we were, it would also make perfect sense that if that was, in fact, 100% what I was smelling.

"Yeah, well, it's not like I know everything," Jane said, rolling her eyes. "How could I have possibly known that there were two of them following us? I swear I only saw one person. The main character generally only needs to deal with *one* creepy stalker sent by the bad guys, in the movies. I mean, that's basically the whole gimmick of the Terminator franchise."

The assailants pulled out guns.

Now we are doubleplus fucked.

Under the assumption that Jane and Albest could take of themselves much better than I ever could in this situation, I turned my attention towards my surroundings, scanning for any signs of life, of someone hiding in the shadows thinking the very thoughts that I was thinking. Now, I wasn't entirely certain whether or not the guys following us were idiots, but under the assumption that they knew what they were doing, it would make sense that a group of three that suddenly became a group of two that suddenly decided to visit the back of a supermarket wasn't a normal situation. The obvious, logical thing to do in this situation was to send two people in to lure out the ambush and then leap in with a pre-emptive strike and then add the relevant attack modifiers to a d20 roll—sorry, my inner D&D nerd took over for a second.

I glanced back at the battle as Albest threw an elbow into the throat of the other guy, who was wearing a black suit and white underwear. How did I know he was wearing white underwear? Well . . . let's just say the suit he was wearing *miiight* have been three sizes too small for him, and the fact that fighting involved, well, a lot of jumping, reaching, and dodging. I saw, unfortunately, way too much of his tighty-whities.

Meanwhile, Jane had just slapped the gun out of the other guy's hands, and he was now fighting with a butterfly knife against an armed librarian, not a good situation, in case you're wondering.

Now, if I was the one doing the ambushing here, I would . . . hide at a corner and stalk around the edges for a while before opening fire; it would be the perfect scenario to properly assess the situation and a more-than-perfect opportunity to snipe my enemies.

Holding my breath, I snuck out of my cover and started making my way towards the nearest dumpster, with a small family of cockroach gathering around it to boot. Scanning the ground, I saw a trail of wet footprints leading to the side. Ducking downwards, I inched forward ever so slowly, not making a sound. But, well, luck has no sympathy for idiots.

Stepping on a slippery piece of rotten tomato, I yelped, almost falling onto the ground, and drawing the attention of everyone towards me. The fight broke up as the two men turned their attention to the shady figure who was standing up from the other side of the dumpster.

I cursed black and blue as I tried to make the best of the situation. Flying forward, I grappled the tall figure on the other side of the dumpster with furious fury.

Noises erupted as he roared and slammed into the ground with considerable force. The side of his head smashed into the bottom of the dumpster with a metallic thud, and he passed out. Blood and drool started coagulating on the ground.

"Wow," I said, surprised. I thought there would have been more of a struggle. Go figure.

"Congratulations, you caught something," Jane

quipped as Albest grabbed a plastic bag and tied it to the two men's heads, before sealing their hands together with discarded packaging wrap he must have scrounged up somewhere.

"Let's hope it's not herpes." I retorted.

Albest made a thoughtful sound. "Jane, that sounded *very* wrong when taken out of context. And Peter? Shame on you for taking there. Shame. Shame. And also, we can't just leave them here."

"You're right. Leaving them out the back of a supermarket that's positively *brimming* with the smell of rotten fish and expired food is just cruel. They deserve to have the dignity to pass out somewhere nice, like, I don't know, a police station or something," Jane said as she symbolically mimed the gesture of holding her hand over her mouth and fanning the other hand in the air as if that would make the place smell any less rancid.

"Hmm, I also agree that the offensive odours covering this place like a damp cloth smell like what would happen when an army of skunks let loose the Big One inside a sewer," Albest said. "But to be honest, I'm not all that thrilled with dragging three unconscious people to the police station. People might think we're criminals or something. Hold on, I'll call Warren."

As one of them mumbled a few words and tried to move his fingertips, Albest swiftly delivered a kick to his groin . . . and he was out like a light again. I shivered fearfully as I felt a tinge of empathy for the guy.

"Hello? Hey, Warren, listen. Could you, get a group of cleaners to come to the parking lot of this Asian supermarket a few blocks away? Yes, that one, with the really smelly bins. Hm? What? No, no, we weren't drunk, no, we were tailed and three men in suits tried to jump us. Nah. We weren't injured. They aren't terribly good at their jobs."

After a few moments of repeating his words to Warren again, Albest hung up the phone. "Yeah, he's sending someone out to pick us up. Let's wait for a while. Pet— Peter? Are you listening? *Hello?* Earth to Peter Stewart, you okay?

I blinked. "Huh? Oh yeah, yeah, sure. I'm okay. Yeah."

Absent-mindedly, I dismissed Albest's questions and rubbed my tired eyes. I thought I saw the silhouette of a man wearing a trench coat pass nearby. But the figure left my vision almost the exact moment that I saw him. Was I seeing things? I quickly dismissed my thoughts and suspicions. It was probably just my tired eyes playing up again.

After all, what kind of person would go to the back of a supermarket wearing a trench coat?

08

AFTER THAT INCIDENT, NO ONE REALLY FELT LIKE

talking. We sat in the back of a minivan and were escorted back to the building with some modicum of dignity intact.

We walked up to the receptionist and I tried to give her a friendly smile. "Excuse me, can you please tell me if Warren is around? There are a few things that we would like to ask him as soon as possible."

The receptionist stared at me expressionlessly for a moment before replying in an even more monotonous voice. "Is it urgent?"

I nodded to silently indicate that, yes, it was

something that we would like to talk about as soon as possible.

She picked up the landline on her desked, put the phone on speaker, pressed one of the speed dial options and started a conversation with Warren's secretary that later forwarded the call to Warren's bodyguard and then was finally forwarded to Warren after ten minutes of shitty music played over the phone as the people working at the call centre tried to assess the validity of the call. She told Warren to come down and talk with us. Turning towards me with flat, emotionless eyes, she said, "The Administrator will be down in a minute. I would appreciate it if you could sit down on the sofa there and wait patiently for his arrival."

We obliged and sat down on the sofa to wait for Warren's arrival. Time passed, and an elevator dinged in the distance as Warren strode out of the elevator before greeting us with a sheepish smile. "M-my apologies for arriving so late. Must've kept you guys waitin.'"

"It's alright," Jane said. "You will have to forgive us for interrupting you so late in the evening, but we just encountered two men who attempted to murder us."

Warren's facial expressions changed so quickly and dramatically that it reminded me of that one guy who always overreacts to things. One minute, he was acting all sheepish and embarrassed, but then his face changed into a complex combination of anger and . . . bloodthirst?

Surprised, I drew back my head sharply and focused on Warren's face again. But the expression disappeared almost as quickly as it appeared.

"Please tell me every detail of what happened. We can't have those annoying flies buzzing around the place, now, can we?" Warren stared down at us with an imposing stare as he, for the first time, looked legitimately intimidating.

With some degree of uncertainty and hesitation, I gestured to Jane to let me take over the conversation and I quickly informed him of what had happened. Warren's face remained stony throughout the entire conversation.

When I finished my description of the events, he said, "I never anticipated them to be so . . . aggressive towards you folks. We will deal with this matter not only because of the concerns for your safety, but also to maintain our integrity as the Human Resistance Against Alien Control."

That was the first time I'd heard someone say the full name of this organisation out loud. It had always been shortened to "the Resistance" or "the organisation" ... and I could see why. The name sounded sooooo stupid. I burst out laughing as I stared back at Warren. The HRAAC sounded like the sound you make when gargling marbles. Not that ... I would know or anything.

"What? Why are you laughing?"

"Never mind," I said, not giving a damn about his somewhat grandiose speech.

"Hm. W-well, I-I-I am cu-curious about exactly wh-what the fuck you guys did to piss those guys off. Normally, they don't go around sending waves after waves of assassins after their targets. The people in the UN and our other partners aren't exactly going to be impressed with this type of action," he said with a hint of curiosity and misplaced interest at Albest, who coughed and attempted to change the conversation.

"Well, I *may have* accidentally, uh, blown up a few major research institutes that can be tied to them through subtle financial trails," Albest said hesitantly while scratching the back of his head. "Okay, and I *might have*, eh, leaked a list of government officials active in our region and some teeny-tiny evidence that could have all of them charged with international terrorism, treason, and crimes against humanity. Well, that, and the whole business of accidentally destroying a supercomputer after downloading seventy-six terabytes of porn onto its hard drive and then switching core program files of the computer with corrupted files of porn." He bit his tongue. "Well, I had a busy year."

Warren's face twitched uncontrollably as he struggled to keep a calm expression while Jane stared coldly at Albest. I was shocked. Honestly, it surprised me just how much damage that guy had managed to do in just one year while running for his life. But then again, that was the guy who figured out how to send a bag of dildos to his best friend without paying a single cent. Truly, a master troll.

At this point, I decided to not even bother reacting to all the crazy shit he claimed to have done last year. I mean, how *was* I supposed to react to something like that? It was so surprising that it didn't even surprise me anymore.

"Um, what did you mean by aliens 'overreaching their authority'?" Jane asked.

Warren attempted to laugh coldly as he said, "The aliens aren't all-powerful. Sure, they have a lot of privileges and authority in many countries. But there's a limit to how outrageous their actions can be. Things like committing mass genocide or sending a small army to wipe out a city, for example, are all actions that are off the table. The financial sinkhole those b-buggers created by sending large numbers of ass-ass-assassins to kill people, well, let's just say there's no s-su-such t-t-t-thing as an infinitely large budget."

"Makes sense," Jane said. "It sort of explains why the assassins they sent after us seemed to be untrained idiots. They *are* untrained idiots." She waved her hand in realisation, accidentally knocking over a cup of water onto the floor, much to the disapproval of Warren.

Warren casually called for Jeremy to clean up the spill. Personally, I thought Jeremy probably held a much more important role here than being a part-time janitor, but Warren insisted that there was a guy whose job it was to clean up after them.

"Well, it was bad PR for both sides," Warren said as he waved Jeremy away. "N-no one likes to t-t-t-talk about them. Not even Cell A."

"Would, uh, the fact that we were almost killed by assassins affect our schedule?" I asked casually. There really wasn't much of a difference whether I worried or not, since I didn't have the ability to defend myself. My life was literally out of my hands.

Throughout my entire life, I was always nothing more than a helpless bystander, and believe me when I say I was content living that way—but that was taken from me. I used to worry about whether or not my family would be affected by my actions and I despised being forced to constantly worry about whether or not I would end up seeing the decomposing remains of my close relatives. I didn't want to felt powerless and I certainly didn't want to end up having a 'Peter Parker meeting Uncle Ben for the last time' moment. Ever.

An organisation as big and powerful as the Resistance must have had the ability to protect their members' families from danger, right? I wanted to believe that, and I thought that might be enough if I continued to work for them and keep them happy.

Warren looked at me in the eye when I said this, and I felt like he *knew* why I asked this question. I felt like he could see the insecurities and fears that I'd been hiding deep inside my heart. That hopeless sense of confusion and distress that I purposefully hid from my friends by feigning a calm and passive personality. The corner of his mouth curled slightly to form a sinister smile. "Why, of course your schedules won't change. After all, why would we allow such a *tiny* thing to impact your schedules? Though, from now on, you will have to be accompanied by a few bodyguards and be kept under surveillance . . . for your sa-safety, but it's all for your own good." His smile deepened. "It is all for your own good."

And then he left.

09

TIME PASSED QUICKLY. AN ENTIRE MONTH WENT BY
without much incident. The day after our quick chat
with him, Warren decided to refurnish our rooms to
make us feel more comfortable living there, though
his offer was declined by Albest and Jane when they
said they were fine with their rooms the way they
were. Albest had attempted to tell me something
during the conversation but was interrupted by a
notification that his schedule had changed due to his
instructor having called in sick. I briefly wondered
what he'd been trying to tell me, before heading off to
receive some self-defence lessons.

Everything had fallen into some semblance of

normality as we settled into our routines. Warren visited to ask how we were doing every once in a while; while, curiously, Jane and Albest avoided him as much as possible. Unfortunately, as much as I wanted to avoid Warren too, he decided to go and find me every time he couldn't find Jane or Albest. So I ended up with the arduous task of talking with him daily and enduring his goddamned stutter.

We didn't meet up as often a few weeks into the course as Jane ended up getting sent to assist Warren sorting files and documents while Albest was sent to work with Jeremy for . . . some reason. I ended up going nowhere, still stuck with my monotonous training schedule to improve my combat and physical abilities.

During my training on weaponry and firearms, I managed to surprise the instructors with how quickly I managed to learn how to handle complicated weapons.

"How did you manage to do it?" he asked. "I thought weapons training was one of hardest courses in basic training." He said this while taking apart a gun and cleaning its insides.

"Never underestimate the hands of a thirty-year-old virgin," I said. "Wizardry isn't the *only* thing we mastered." This elicited a small laugh from him.

Then we returned to punching practise. And I stopped laughing.

On the other hand, I also had that temp job at the shitty office space that the Resistance cleared out for me to work in. So, naturally, I spent the better part of my days looking bored and taking phone calls. On the rare occasion that I found a person who I had the security clearance to talk to and eavesdrop on . . . things got interesting. Perhaps the most memorable phone call that I had was for a field agent called Jomés Brondstein, who probably confused way too many bartenders with his requests to mix martinis with diet Pepsi, Vodka, and lemon juice, by the way (and if you point out that any and all requests to mix an alcoholic beverage with diet Pepsi, Vodka, and lemon juice as a part of its recipe is not only an insult to your taste buds, but to the bartender, who actually has to mix those drinks, as well . . . then you are probably correct on both counts. Also, diet Pepsi should not be mixed with alcoholic beverages). The guy spent a worryingly large amount of time abusing his privileges of having access to the large treasure trove of personal data that the Resistance had collected over the years by calling up the IT department to help check on the social media accounts and medical records of his latest dates with the flimsy excuse of "Hey, mon, gathering info, I'm gathering info". I assure you, I was eating popcorn throughout the entire conversation, as with several others, who had put their own calls on hold to eavesdrop on Bronstein's conversations. I don't think he realised that call operators like me have the right to record and listen in on his phone calls and that we don't usually drop the call immediately after we connect their calls with whomever they happened to wish to speak to.

Jomés Brondstein quickly ended up becoming one of my few sources of entertainment throughout the week as I ended up receiving at least thirteen different calls from him requesting to talk the IT department regarding at least seven different unresolved incidents of unprofessional conduct during field operations. It really made me wonder how he had ever managed to finish a mission with him being so hell-bent on contaminating the world's gene pool with his DNA. I never did know how the seven cases were resolved, but I had a few guesses. One of them involved a shark tank and another involved castration—neither of which would be pleasant things to happen to you. We did chat every now and then as the calls connected. It was a nice bit of entertainment.

Warren came by to congratulate me when I

finally completed my two month induction period, and invited me to a small party on the other side of the town so I could "relax after two months of monotonous exercises, man" . . . or so he said. He may also have been high at the time. After two months of staying with him, I realised that he had a serious drug problem.

The party was hosted at the nearby mansion of some random person whose name I forgot the minute my eyes left the pamphlet advertising said party. No one gives a shit about the hosts anyway, no matter how large they print their names. The party animals are there only to get drunk and dry hump each other as they attempt to dance. Hosting a party will very likely leave your house trashed, filled with empty liquor bottles and broken dreams and someone's first time. I heard rumours that you might find dirty condoms where you least expect them to be.

Ah yes, I derailed and went off-topic again, didn't I? Apologies, let's get back to the story. As I stepped out of the car, I also saw Jane and Wu Er drinking a shit-ton of beer at the furthest edge of the yard. I took a deep breath before walking towards them, grabbing a can of beer from some guy on the way. I urged my mouth to form a smile.

"Hey guys," I said awkwardly. "It's been a while since we've hung out."

"It sure has." Wu Er gave a friendly chuckle, while Jane rolled her eyes. "So, let's talk more then, Peter. How are you finding this place?"

"It's okay, I suppose. Where's—"

"Where's Albest?" Jane asked, joining me in an off-pitched harmony.

I frowned. "It's been two months. The first time his schedule changed, I thought nothing of it. But I haven't seen him since." I suddenly felt nervous, more than I had felt in a long time.

Wu Er and Jane exchanged a nervous look with each other. Jane looked slightly teary as she slammed down another bottle of beer. After a good helping of the liquid courage, she made eye contact with me. "Peter, I thought you knew. We haven't seen him in *weeks*. The last time we saw him, he said he was going to have a talk with you."

"Goddammit, that happened ages ago," I said. "He didn't show up because he said his schedule changed. I thought he was paired with one of you. It's not like we live next door or anything." I struggled to breathe. What happened to him?

"Well," Wu Er said, carefully, as though he wasn't sure how to phrase this. "I never saw him much, but I remember seeing him around my workplace a little more than a week ago. I was doing night shifts, doing a stocktake of all the ampules of Dioxin-based compounds we have on-hand and I remember seeing him there."

A slight flicker of hope bubbled up in me. "What? Really?"

"Yeah, that's why I wasn't really worried at first. But . . . something's wrong. He . . . wasn't supposed to be there. At least, I don't remember Warren granting him any security clearance."

"Your . . . workplace. Isn't that *the Building*?" I said, slightly nervous. If Albest was doing what I thought he was doing there, well, I didn't like his odds. "Can you take us there?"

Wu Er looked nervous as well, avoiding eye contact. "Look, I don't know. The place is closed now. I probably shouldn't have seen him there either. But . . . you know how it is here. Something's not right about this place, and I might get referred to HR if I get caught telling too much, that wouldn't mesh well with Warren's idea of what is and what isn't need-to-know."

"Mister Wu Er, I get what you're feeling," Jane said. "Thanks for telling us this much already. We'll take it from here. Just . . . don't tell Warren what we're going to do next."

A panic flashed over his eyes. "And what are you going to do next?"

She averted his gaze, fidgeting with her hands, and with her voice barely audible over the booming party music surrounding us, said, "Nothing. Absolutely nothing."

Wu Er laughed bitterly. Jane slammed the bottle onto the table, spilling beer in the process. And the mood worsened into an uncomfortable stale mate.

"What do you want, Mister Wang?" Jane asked again, with a firmer voice this time.

". . . I want nothing to do with this." He cringed.

"Because of you, Albest might die. You know him, too. Doesn't that matter to you?" Jane continued, carefully trying to control her emotions.

He closed his eyes, and drew a deep breath before finally downing half a can of cheap beer. "Well, let's just say I get myself drunk early on in the night and I have no recollection of what's going to happen next. Toast?"

"Yeah, let's toast," I agreed hurriedly, afraid that he might change his mind.

We raised a sloppy toast, and Wu Er sighed. "Let's leave."

"Yep. Let's go save Albest," Jane said, a hint of cheerfulness returning to her voice.

"Hold on, who said anything about me helping you save Albest?" He stared impassively at us, before half-heartedly dodging an empty beer can that I 'accidentally' threw towards his face—which elicited a high-pitched yelp that I promptly ignored. "So, you're saying that we infiltrate a behemoth of an organisation that is being run by an anonymous group of people powerful enough to subvert, oh let's see, *the eyes and ears of basically every single major political force on the planet* and find one guy because of a random thing that I said. Two questions: When was the last time you heard of a case where the CEO of a company tells the night janitor every single one of his corporate secrets? And how the ever-loving *fuck* would I know where to find him? He might very well be out of the city. It's as likely a possibility as anything else. Without enough information, we'll just be trying to find a shave of gold in the desert. I'll help you enter, sure, but I'm definitely not helping you do anything else."

". . . Good enough for now," Jane conceded, sighing.

I rubbed my temples. God, I felt like the longer I stayed there, the more frequent my headaches became. After taking a shaky breath, I said, "Well, that's great. I feel so much more reassured now." The corner of my mouth twitched convulsively as I struggled to keep my smile. I drank a few swigs of beer to compose myself. "Guys, we are all sorta-drunk. Are we seriously planning to go and break into a heavily guarded place *while drunk*? Can't we do this tomorrow?"

"I have a work shift tomorrow," Wu Er said. "Today's the only day I'm free, and besides, it is precisely because I'm drunk that I'm agreeing with you right now. In no other situation would I ever agree to go do something as crazy as this."

"Why are you implying that *I'm* drunk? I'm perfectly sober!" Jane said. "I can count all the way to ten! Besides, I'm sure they'll understand our excuses of being drunk and accidentally getting lost on the way to find the toilet!" Jane waved the beer bottles at me. I flinched, not entirely sure whether I would be forced to dodge a beer bottle soon.

Wu Er shrugged. "We'll make it up as we go. Listen, here's what we're going to do . . ."

After five more minutes of arguing, drinking, and some more drinking, I reluctantly agreed to a crazy but somewhat thought-out plan that we collectively concocted in a drunken haze. In detail. It was a terrible plan, probably. Whatever. I feel like the world is spinning out of balance and I think I am now officially stupid enough to agree to this crazy plan!

All I could hope was that I didn't regret this decision once I sobered up. Though, thankfully, Jane drunk less beer than myself and was probably capable of making the right decisions. God, I hoped she was.

10

WE LEFT THE PARTY WITHOUT ALERTING ANYONE

and then proceeded to head towards—cue dramatic thunder and lightning—*the Building*. If I said I wasn't nervous, then I would be lying. I literally had cold sweat trickling down my back like a tiny water fountain and was beginning to heavily regret every single life decision I'd ever made.

A familiar building appeared in front of me. Concrete on all sides, hardened cement slabs for ground, with a tall indomitable fence surrounding it. There were no key holes nor a pin pad. The sign on the side said it was the administrative office of a bank, but to be honest, we all knew better at this point.

"Not this way," Wu Er said as he dragged me away from the building to the side of a plain and uninteresting alleyway.

"Where are we going?" I asked.

"To the password-protected emergency exit." He sighed. "I really don't want to do this, but here we go."

He knelt down and started feeling his way around the bricks. Eventually he grunted and pressed a hidden switch for an alphanumeric keypad to appear on the walls.

"Every once in a while, some idiot forgets to bring his identification card to work. Cell PX-300456 recently spent a tenth of their R&D budget to connect the secret keypad gimmick and get it to work," Wu Er said, shrugging, as he looked at me with a mocking smile. "What? You think I would use my own identification card to bring you guys into the building?"

"Okay, so I was wrong. You don't have to act like a dick about it."

"Sorry what? I didn't catch the last part."

"Never mind," I said, as Wu Er pulled out his phone.

"Hello? Resistance call centre?" Wu Er whispered secretively, I winced. There was probably a dozen bored workers tuning into his convo right now. Let's hope he didn't give away anything too critical to the plan before we even enter the building. "Can you redirect my call to, yeah, yeah, Keeper of Passwords, is he awake? Oh. Oh. He's currently hunting down a beast with two back and performing the horizontal tango? Wha—oh he fucking? Damn. You're putting me on hold until he finishes? Fuck you."

A muted series of shitty jazz music and poorly placed advertisement placed from Wu Er's phone as I heard him mutter a curse in Chinese and paced around nervously. The whole 'keeper of passwords' thing felt like a terrible idea precisely because of situations like this. Only after another five minutes of nervous waiting and pacing around, the call finally connected, Wu Er inputted a series of alphanumeric combinations that took him almost an entire minute as a heavy voice guided him on.

He pulled opened the door with a click, motioning us to go inside.

A long, narrow hallway stretched out before me. There were no stairs, just a gradually-inclining slope with a tacky black-on-yellow 'NOW SUPPORTING WHEELCHAIR AND QUADRIPLEGIC ACCESS' sign on the right-hand side of the wall. I . . . Frankly, I had no idea quadriplegics worked there.

It was an ugly hallway. I suppose. The place wasn't

beautiful; no, the place was beautiful in much the same way you would consider the mutilated bodies of serial killer victims 'beautiful' or 'artistic'. In fact, to take the analogy one step further, I would say that this entire goddamned architecturally-disjointed place was the combined effort of two different serial killers piecing together their victims to form one horrific whole.

Hey, did I mention I was drunk yet?

The hallway was uncomfortably narrow, to the point that we had to move forward single-file. The wall on the left was made of some sort of metal that I couldn't identify while the right side was made of wood, and the floor was made of bricks. The hallway itself was tilted at an uncomfortable angle that caused the walls to graze my shoulders as I walked. The overhead lighting was, unfortunately, blue fluorescent lights that lit up the emergency exit like a heavy-metal rave.

I watched as I saw some scuttling beetles migrating around the room. I groaned. Those blasted pests were nearly the size of my fist. Holy hell did this place suck.

Wu Er scratched his head in embarrassment. "Yeah, I don't quite remember the emergency exits being this bad. I thought the pest control department dealt with the bug infestation ages ago. Most of the surface inspections revealed no foreign germs or insect prints. This isn't right."

"Can the Resistance not hire competent architects or something?" Jane sniped as she accidentally bumped into the walls for the fourth time in a row.

" . . . Warren was the lead architect for the project," Wu Er said. "He reasoned that, well, since he's the Administrator of cell PX-300456, he gets to do whatever the fuck he wants with the assigned budget. He, uh, he said something about modelling it after a vivid dream that he had when he was a kid."

"That," Jane paused, "explains so much. Suddenly, everything makes sense."

We took a collective sigh of exasperation as we marched onwards and finally exited the emergency exit area and entered the building proper without alerting anyone to our presence.

Wu Er stopped in front of us, somewhat shocked as he turned around in bewilderment. "Sweet mother of God! Slap me."

Jane slapped him.

"OW! What the f— What did you do that for?" Wu Er yelped in pain for a second, before quickly realising that we were supposed to be stealthy. So instead, he hissed angrily at Jane.

"Hey, you asked me to slap you," she responded

defensively, looking around in the hopes of finding someone to help her justify the fact that she had just slapped Wu Er.

"I meant that as a figure of speech," he snarled, rubbing his cheeks vigorously. "Well, at least it wasn't that bad, I guess."

"You didn't sound like you were kidding around. You seriously sounded like you were asking for it."

"Guys, guys," I interjected. "I know we aren't exactly the best of friends, but can we focus on what we had planned and head to the control room already?"

That's right. Our plan was simple. As the entire place was riddled with those fancy-schmancy next-gen security systems, all of the security footage was automatically categorised by some computer system with procedurally-generated tags given to each sequence of security footage. The entire process was apparently implemented because some high-level idiot had, at some point, lost their car keys here and, rather than calling their insurance numbers, they had chosen to instead (ab)use their privilege to get some poor soul working the security guard shift to help him retrace his entire day using the security camera system to find them (spoiler: he left it in his office), and after more than three hours of poring through security footage, he vowed to take the complaint to Warren.

As a member of the higher management, he was very well-received by Warren and, as such, he'd quickly managed to sell him on the idea of installing a new security system that came with its own internal search engine.

It was a stupid-simple plan, but a plan's a plan. And I thought we should stick to it.

Wu Er shook his head, looking around again in amazement. "Somehow, I've never been to this part of the building before. I'm officially bamboozled. That emergency exit was, apparently, the wrong emergency exit. Jeez, they really should just, you know, *label the emergency exits*. We may have travelled up the wrong emergency exit and now, uh, we may be hopelessly lost."

"WHAT!!?" Jane and I recoiled in surprise. "You're the head of staff or scientists or whatever around here. How could you get lost in the very building you supervise? That's literally half your job description. Would the president of the United States get lost inside the White House? Do you think this would ever happen?"

"Look, as embarrassing as this sounds, I'm being honest right now, and I've never been to this place before. The bleeding heck is this place? And where are the cameras?" Wu Er furrowed his eyebrows. "Why aren't there any security cameras in this area? Awful! According to Section 4-03 of the Resistance Standard Protocol, a security camera must be installed at every corner of a Resistance-owned building. This is *highly improper.*"

He ranted for a while before he fanned his face in exasperation. "Okay, we just need to find a familiar area or some sort of location identifier within the building and I should be able to get you guys the hell out of this weird place."

We collectively decided that we wanted to leave this creepy place behind. I innocently thought that absolutely nothing could go wrong now that we had someone who knew the building layout with us to help us prowl through the building looking for some trace of where Albest had disappeared to—but remember, kids, never tempt fate to prove you wrong; the Universe hates getting tested.

Seriously, I literally just saw a door leading to nowhere and a few dozen hallways that curved inwards and outwards and then back around in an S-shape.

"Well, at least I'm familiar with the overall building scheme," Wu Er said, latching onto some shred of positive news to stay optimistic in this situation. "If my understanding of the building is correct, then we could just go on a slow and leisurely walk down the hallway to our left, make another left-turn at some point, and then we *should* be out of unfamiliar territory and back into the parts of the building that I know."

"Hold on a second. If you don't know jack about this area of the building, how do you know exactly how we can get out of here?" Jane asked with a slightly accusing tone.

"Well, as someone who has worked here for a long time, I know enough about the building's layout to deduce roughly where this secret area is in relation to the rest of the building. Remember, we entered from the right-hand side of the building and headed up a staircase. So, we should be east of the control room, which is close to the lounge and on the first floor of the building." Wu Er didn't even bother to disguise his irritation as his voice crept higher. "Now, as I have said, this will be a piece of cake. So just sit back and relax—"

Fortunately, a loud siren that echoed through the entire facility interrupted Wu Er's sentence. Unfortunately, *a loud siren* that echoed throughout the entire facility interrupted Wu Er's sentence. There were only two possibilities for this: either our first (and possibly the last) attempt into the often-fatal field of espionage was discovered or someone else is trying the exact same thing as we are. Either scenario meant we were knee-deep in some thick green shit.

11

"ATTENTION! ATTENTION!" A MECHANICAL VOICE
blared over the speakers. *"Containment breach from
cell X-0004 on floor -1. Initiating automated nonlethal
containment procedure 4 . . . Initiation of nonlethal
containment procedure 4 failed. All security personnel
are to gather on floor -1!"*

"I'm sorry, but I *swear* you were just saying
something. Mind repeating it?" Jane snapped at Wu
Er. Apparently, she was not feeling any happier than I
was, but then again, most people wouldn't be feeling
very cheerful in this situation.

". . . I stand corrected," Wu Er finally said,
breathing out. "Oh man, what I wouldn't give to be

someone that's riding a Segway through the city's night market, completely oblivious to everything that's going on here right now."

"Well, you would be arrested for drink driving," Jane pointed out. "If there's one thing that you're not: it is sober."

"Hang on." I frowned. "Can you get arrested for riding a Segway while intoxicated?"

"Not the point," Jane said, dodging the question. Then: "I'll search it up on Bing later."

We ran down the hallways and found ourselves facing a very conspicuous elevator. There were probably security cameras inside there and, because it made sense in our drunken minds at that particular moment in time, we took off our jackets and tied them around our faces in an attempt to hide . . . I'll admit that idea made more sense to me when I was drunk.

"You know, maybe it would be a good idea to apply some makeup to disguise our faces as well. Just to, you know, make double sure that we don't get caught," Wu Er said.

"Wait, you have a makeup bag with you?" I said.

"Of course I do. I thought I would be attending one of those *fuuucked-up* parties tonight. Shame that I got side-tracked, but yes, I brought some makeup with me. You gonna ask questions?" he snapped, looking at me with a hint of embarrassment as well. I mean, I could plausibly believe that he would be the kind of guy to bring weird stuff to a party.

The elevator doors opened with a ding. We had enough sense within us to wait for a while to examine the buttons. There were only four of them, fortunately, so that whittled down the margin of error by quite a bit. One of the buttons was helpfully labelled 'Ground floor'; another was labelled 'Office area', which was probably where the control room was, and that would be where we needed to go to find the footage of what happened to Albest. The third button was simply labelled 'Ω', there was no indication of what that floor contained, but I quickly decided that we were not going there. The fourth button was, uh, interesting to say the least. It was placed away from the other three buttons, with the number -1 engraved into it and a plaque beneath it in familiar black-on-yellow layout, reading: AUTHORISED PERSONNEL ONLY.

"So, are we going to . . . head upwards? Higher than the ground floor?" Jane asked, rubbing her eyes in a daze.

"Just press the button." Could my day get any worse? Now the elevator started playing elevator music, which happened to have a repetitive two-bar melody that was more annoying than happy. The tune hammered itself into my head.

Jane pressed the button. The elevator moved.

Downwards.

"Wait, what the fuck? Why are we going downwards?" Jane muttered.

"Someone must have called it below us," Wu Er said.

An oppressing atmosphere of silence filled the elevator.

Shitty elevator music blared over the speakers. It sounded like an unholy mixture of the classic too-happy Disney music and reggae jazz, which can really ruin mood of anyone who is forced to listen to it while pondering the possibility of their imminent mortality.

Wu Er's phone buzzed. He flicked it open and stared at it for a very long time. He froze on the spot, his face going pale with a visceral fear that made him look like he was going to spontaneously shit his pants. "Ah. Shit, I think we should put on the makeup, you know . . . some disguises to make sure that we don't caught. That okay with you?"

"Yeah, sure, let's get to it," I muttered.

The elevator dinged, and the doors slid open on Floor -1.

You know, the place that we were explicitly told *not* to go to in helpful black-on-yellow layout, complete with an atrociously awful serif. As someone who has worked on his fair share of PowerPoint presentations and formatting office reports for the majority of his life, I can tell you that the font was somehow a more atrocious version of Comic Sans. A white-hot seething rage boiled inside me, growing hotter the longer I stared at the warning. It wasn't even aligned to the middle and justified. Oh yeah, and there's something shitty going on down there, but I honestly care more about the atrocious serifs!

The doors slid open, revealing an impatient figure on the other side of the door. I gulped. He was wearing a mesh mask over his entire head that covered him so thoroughly that it was impossible to tell who it was that was staring back at us. It could have been anyone, really. From head to toe, the man donned thick animal-handling clothing with a utility belt so chock-full of nonlethal physical and chemical restraints that it put Batman to shame.

Shrinking back into myself, I hoped feverishly that he wouldn't recognise me. I thought my odds were good, as I looked almost nothing like I did two months ago—and that's before you take into consideration the heavy makeup and the jacket around my face.

"Who?" the man murmured, his voice muffled by the headgear.

He sounded . . . familiar.

Wu Er gave a laugh as we casually walked outside. "Ah, we are friends of Warren. You know, from Warren's, uh, whatchamacallit weekend non-profit-thingy camp for socially stigmatised youth and adults."

"Huh. Socially stigmatised adults." He gave us the once over, before snorting in derision. Well, we looked the part. "Clearance? Not a good time to be here for a tour. The containment breach will make short of the security personnel here. You'll be in danger."

"Of course. Of course. Obviously, Warren gave us *clearance*." Wu Er spoke rapidly, expertly. "Lü Guo. Pleased to meet you."

"Code," the armoured man said.

"PX-300456," Wu Er said without blinking.

Nodding, he examined us (I assume) with a friendly look and continued, "Then you will need to get a set of protective gear from the changing room down the corridor to my right. You should see a beautiful red door there. You just need to turn the lock in."

"Hahahaha, that's a good joke." Wu Er laughed nervously. I saw a hint of cold sweat sliding down his neck as he continued, a slight shakiness creeping into his voice. "We all know that there's nothing to the right of anything labelled 0002 since the doors face each other diagonally...right? Ohgodpleasetellmeimright. Hahahaha, besides, there's not a trace of red anywhere within this facility—totally against Warren's obsession with the colour blue. The logical fallacy of turning a lock inward...Oh, this is *so funny*. A-are you reaching for the spray?"

"Oh, of course not," the man guffawed, easing his grip on the can of chemical spray. "Always nice to find someone who appreciates a good joke. Now, time's running out. Show me your ID cards."

We fell silent. There were no ID cards—well, none that we could show him without incriminating ourselves, anyway. We aren't supposed to be here. We were supposed to be at the party, drunk and wasting away on a couch whilst regretting every decision that we'd ever made.

"We don't have IDs," I accidentally blurted out. If eyes could kill, there'd be two funerals next week for the two halves of my body—the one that Jane killed and the one that Wu Er killed. I tried my best not to move. The armoured man slowly pulled out the can of chemical restraints and held it in our direction. "W-wait, listen to me. This was a misunderstanding!" I stammered. "We don't have IDs because we are, uh, part of the, um, secret operation. Yes! Yes! You idiot, you almost jeopardised our whole operation!"

If I could peek under his helmet, I'm sure he would've looked as confused as Jane and Wu Er combined. But what was I supposed to do? I needed to make some shit up that was so ass-bewilderingly crazy that it might actually have been believable!

"S-sorry?" he said, holding his pepper spray as I channelled Steve's drill sergeant impression.

"WE ARE IN THE PROCESS OF A SECRET INSPECTION OF THIS FACILITY, MAGGOT. WHAT YOU JUST DID WAS UNACCEPTABLE! ACCORDING TO SECTION 2 OF THE EMPLOYEE CODE, YOU WERE SUPOPOSED TO SHOOT FIRST AND ASK QUESTIONS LATER SHOULD YOU SEE THREE UNIDENTIFIED INDIVIDUALS GOING DOWN THE ELEVATOR IN AN EMERGENCY SITUATION." Drama class was really paying off, I thought with some relief as I hissed angrily at a completely random stranger. "THERE'S NO TIME TO CONFIRM WHETHER PEOPLE LIKE US ARE HERE IN ANY OFFICIAL CAPACITY IN

A SITUATION LIKE THIS! IMAGINE HOW YOU WOULD'VE BEHAVED IN A *REAL* EMERGENCY."

"B-b-but I thought this was a real emergency," the tinny voice emerging from inside the armour replied, sounding like it was on the verge of tears. I reckon he had a traumatic experience interacting with Steve as well, then.

"IT WAS ONLY THE NONLETHAL CONTAINMENT CELL X-0004, WHICH IS, LIKE, BASICALLY A DRILL, MAGGOT!" I rasped, mostly because my voice probably couldn't take the strain of more yelling. I pulled out my phone, which had the recording button turned on. "Now, I have recorded this entire conversation of you pathetic maggot wasting our time and disobeying basic protocols. Do you want us, the secret superintendents, to report this grave offence to your superior?"

He shook his head rapidly. "No sir, no. I'll be on my way to address the emergency now."

As he walked off, we quickly ducked away in case he decided to change his mind mid-run. After we made sure that there were no other complications to be dealt with, we breathed a collective sigh of relief.

"Oh god, I thought we were going to be caught for sure," Wu Er said, sounding light-headed as he spoke, words tripping over each other in an attempt to escape his mouth. "Luckily we have a shitty boss and a shittier squad of security. Never have I been more grateful to be working for an incompetent asshole who hired a group of gullible security guards."

"Hey, that was a pretty amazing performance," Jane said. "Have you ever considered becoming an actor?"

I chuckled nervously for a few seconds. "Well, it certainly helped that the person I was speaking to was pretty gullible, and the fact that the only training instructor here just happened to be the most outrageously stereotypical drill instructor-type asshole that I have ever seen. Half of them probably still have some psychological wounds from dealing with that guy. I know *I* do."

The underground area wasn't part of our orientation tour. And also, apparently a good quarter of this entire building was entirely hidden from Wu Er's eyes, which . . . wasn't helpful. We tried to make sense of exactly what the purpose of this floor was, exploring as many rooms as possible until we managed to stumble into what appeared to be a large testing area.

It was a pristine work area of one-way mirrors, dozens upon dozens of computer monitors lined up on one wall. I peered into the one-way mirror.

No reflection. Must have been facing the other way. I looked closer and saw a . . . Roomba moving innocuously inside. As it noticed our presence, the machine trundled through a small vent and entered the room.

Wu Er widened his eyes in shock. "Mah Gah! That's HICKLER-1! I thought it was only a rumour! The testing facility for the HICKLER prototype was down here all along!"

"Really? You're going to be surprised by a fucking Roomba right now? And also, that was the dumbest and most unrealistic line that I've heard. Ever. I feel like you're just gradually devolving into a shitty parody of yourself with every passing minute."

"Hey," Wu Er protested weakly. "I'm stressed."

"We're all stressed," I shot back, feeling another headache coming on.

As far as I could tell, only one of the monitors was actually active. It displayed a bunch of numbers that kept changing and fluctuating in a seemingly random manner. However, as I looked closer, I realised that the incomprehensible numbers appeared to be coordinates of some sort. Another monitor showed an atrocious computer program that seemed to be designed by a deranged programmer high on caffeine, with the worst user interface that I had ever seen slathered over the screen in all its awful, awful, glory.

"What the hell is this?" I asked in a state of half-disbelief.

"Holy shit," Wu Er squeezed out as he looked at the area where the door used to be. "The rumours were true all along. So that's why I never found the place."

The coordinates displayed on the screen seemed to correspond with the directions the mechanical objected seemed to move in . . . At least, that's what I would assume, anyway. The colour palette for the display was so monochromatic that even the simple action of discerning what was on the goddamned screen was difficult. The designer seemed to have abandoned interest in finishing any lasting patches that would've made it easier to read halfway through the program as numerous windows showing the same information started flashing up. The crème-de-la-crème, of course, was a looping three-frame animation of a flashing pirate flag skull-and-crossbones with the words '133t sh1z 1n pr0gr3ss.'

That line was also written in Comic Sans.

My palm rose up to meet my forehead. I groaned as I tried focusing on the key information displayed onscreen. "I'm guessing the Resistance spent all of their dough on covering up their secret lab and then forgot to assign any of the remainder to the programming department. Or the design department, from the looks of it."

"Agreed," Jane grunted.

"Or it could've been design by Warren." Wu Er stated, proposing an awful answer to an awful situation.

Sounds of footsteps thundered in the distance. It wouldn't be a good idea for us to keep wandering around at this point. I doubted we could bluff our way past another group of security guards if we kept this up. It was only because of pure dumb luck that we had managed to survive thus far anyways. I wasn't going to push my luck.

Wu Er locked the entrances to the room and, breathed raggedly, said, "What do we do now? We're pretty darned trapped, and we essentially have no way of effectively exploring this place with the guards soon to be flooding every corner."

Jane sat down. "Seriously. It's getting dangerous. I don't know what the hell they're talking about when it comes to containment breaches and all that jazz, but I do know that we're pretty much screwed if we don't get out of here. To make matters worse, we would be leaving *empty-handed.* Another opportunity like this isn't going to come by again."

Ignoring Wu Er, she turned her eyes to meet mine. "Peter, what do you think? We stay, or we leave as soon as possible and do all the crazy stuff another day?"

I avoided eye contact. My instinct told me to run as far away from this place as possible at the first possible moment. But doing so would be counter-intuitive and carried its own risks.

If I were to weigh my option without context, a containment breach meant the attention of the guards would be stretched thin enough for us to investigate further, but this whole containment breach thing also implied that there would be more security pouring in until the incident was resolved. As far as I could tell, the alarm hadn't been turned off yet, which meant whatever it was they were dealing with was still an ongoing issue as of that moment. The chances of us bumping into another guard or an armed security on our way out was high enough to be a near-certainty. Conversely, this also meant that whatever escaped its confinement was dangerous enough to warrant such attention. I didn't know what it was they had contained there, but I doubted it was sunshine and lollipops. Trapping ourselves also made us vulnerable to be discovered by the security, and the probability of that happening was directly proportional to the amount of time we spent locked inside that room.

But anyway, back to Jane's question. "We stay until we find something."

Seemingly satisfied with this answer, Jane nodded. "Well, as Wu Er said, investigating this place in a situation like this is still dangerous and our options will be very limited in terms of exploring this entire facility. It seems so . . . hopeless. If only there was some way of investigating this place without inadvertently placing ourselves in danger every time we take a step forward."

I stared at the glitchy monitor screen showing the shitty programmed display and its menu, then turned my eyes to HICKLER-1, the wannabe Roomba that was in the process of cleaning up the dirty footprints that we tracked in with a vigorous zeal that I could only describe as "anger-induced cleaning obsession."

A smile crept over my face. "Hold that thought. I think I have an idea."

12

HICKLER-1 TRUNDLED DOWN THE HALLWAY SILENTLY,
the hum of its engine and clashing against the other
background noises should have made it completely
imperceptible to the ear. The weaponised vacuum
cleaner was completely ignored by everyone. After all,
what was a vacuum cleaner in all that pandemonium
anyways?

The camera feed gave us a shot of frenzied feet
stomping down in one direction or another. It took
us more than five minutes to figure out how to turn
on the camera because of a bug in the programming
that spat out an error message in elvish every time
we tried to turn it on. Fortunately, Jane was a

librarian and part-time Tolkienian scholar who had a more-than-passing understanding of Sindarin, the elvish language of Middle-earth. Together, we deciphered the error message and debugged the danged program from a console . . . By we, I mean we muttered words of encouragement and offered pats on the back while she did the hard work of scribbling out the error message, deciphered the intended message, and wrote out the translated version and directives for Warren to debug. Through our combined, uh, team effort, the screen flickered and a window containing a live feed from a hidden camera attached to the tiny robot appeared.

We made a tiny whoop of accomplishment and gave each other high-fives despite the fact that we did exactly zero percent of the hard work. But that was hardly the point now, was it?

The robot vacuum cleaner was good to go, and so we sent it out to do the dirty work for us.

Our original intention was to simply get our hands on security footage that would lead us to Albest, but with everything that had transpired thus far, I'd reckon we were all more than inclined to agree that some serious shit was going on, and I had a feeling Albest may have very well been on that very floor, knee-deep in the involvement with that deep dark doo-doo.

The fact that Floor -1 was only accessible by a secret elevator that denied access (*attempted* to deny access) to anyone who wasn't authorised personnel was telling. I got the feeling that whoever designed this place wasn't exactly too keen on the idea of subtlety. Mostly because of the fact this entire place was built with about as much care and subtlety as an axe-murder.

Observing the world through the camera feed, we saw a tiny corridor filled with refractive lasers, security cameras, and AK-47s attached to the aforementioned cameras. At the end of the hallway was a dented reinforced-steel door with a sign on the doorknob reading: 'DO NOT ENTER. ABSOLUTELY NOTHING SUSPICIOUS OR RELEVANT INSIDE THIS DOOR. AND *DEFINITELY* NO PRISONERS'. The sign was also written in comic-sans.

The flooring changed from the signature white marble tiles to a familiar series of wooden planks that I'd seen on the ground floor of the R&D building and within the training area of the office building. There was a keypad stuck on the wall.

Feedback from HICKLER-1 appeared on the monitor, informing us of a foreign contaminant that was made up of about 55% water, amounts of glucose, trace amounts of oxygen and carbon dioxide, and various other chemical elements. A quick search on Bing revealed ... a weblink to fructose syrup, and a blog dedicated to someone's missing pet. So, we did the next best thing: have a group discussion. We concluded that the dried stains trailing on the floor were probably blood, and I was quite sure how to feel about that.

"Wow. Overkill, much?" I looked at it in resignation. It was so obviously suspicious and conspicuous that I felt like my IQ was insulted by its very presence.

Jane used the sophisticated camera controls to take a closer look at the thing—meaning she did some redundant button-mashing in accordance to a confusing sketch of an anatomically incorrect Vitruvian Man. We assumed the arms and legs and the ... very, very, very generously drawn male member were representative of directions the camera could pivot and zoom in on, since there were keyboard buttons where the hands, feet, and, uh, 'tip' of the subject should've been. After a few awkward experiments at controlling camera angles and the zoom, we got it down under. Unfortunately, we haven't yet figured out how to close the window of the camera control guide at that moment in time. I assure you that image was eye poison.

Cold sweat flowed down Jane's neck like a waterfall as she gently guided the damned thing through the criss-crossing maze of lasers and security cameras. Fortunately, evading the lasers was that much easier as we had a size advantage; the Roomba-wannabe was only ten or so centimetres tall, and, as you may or may not have noticed, not a human being. It easily evaded the traps that were obviously intended to keep *humans* out.

As the machine bumped into the steel door, the already heavily damaged steel door just . . . collapsed on itself and fell down. Good news: we didn't have to worry about the door anymore. Bad news: the door also crushed HICKLER-1.

As we stared blankly for a second, I coughed. "Well, at least we have a clear direction of where we need to go next. Now, what do you think could have been capable of creating those fist-shaped dents in the steel doors. I mean, I could be wrong, but I am almost certain that the door was dented by fists."

"I don't know," Jane replied. "Let's go down there and check what's inside. The door was dented inwards, so the door wasn't damaged from inside the room. We shouldn't encounter too many risks if we stick to the safe route and then go see what the hell is inside. The trail of blood definitely means that it's probably a person who's locked inside."

As the three of us reached an agreement, we headed off to the very conspicuous hallway filled with AK-47s attached to security cameras.

After an intense session of jogging, I stopped to catch my breath. Within minutes, we had found ourselves standing in front of the heavily-guarded hallway again. Only, this time, the traps and the lasers were deactivated, and the cameras were pointing downwards at the ground. It didn't really make much sense if you think too heavily about it. Just because the steel door collapsed, it doesn't mean every other part of the security system will stop working. I touched the side of the steel frame. Warm. The metal was warm to touch, almost.

I slowly shuffled towards the darkened abyss that was barely contained by the steel door. I stepped over the fallen steel door and a sinking felting tugged at me in my gut. An unnameable dread rose up within me. I gulped.

There was absolutely nothing inside the room except the trail of blood leading outside. I cursed, and looked at Jane and Wu Er as I said the obvious:

"Whoever was here has already left. Let's follow the trail and see where it leads."

"Sure. Sounds like an idea," Jane admitted, and we followed the trail of blood, eventually arriving outside what looked like a decaying broom closet, with the door frame rotted to the point that it looked like just touching it would give you splinters. Again, this didn't really make sense when you compared it to everything else within the building. The dull, wooden finish actually made it look *more* suspicious with how outlandish the rest of the building looked.

With my heart pounding, I pushed open the door. As I expected, the door wasn't locked. An ingenious deduction on my part, if I have to say so. Unfortunately, what happened afterwards just devolved into senseless nightmare fuel.

"What. The. Fuck," I said in shock at the contents of the room—and that was not a compliment. I surveyed the room with a mixture of horror and awe.

This room did not share any resemblance to the other rooms in the facility. It was sterile clean, yet the entire place made me feel like it might as well have been covered in caterpillars and cockroaches. It was clean, yet dirty at the same time . . . Does that make sense? You would have to excuse me. It was pretty difficult for me to describe the place precisely as I wasn't necessarily focused on the architecture of the room in that moment.

The room smelled of formaldehyde and various other preservatives, while the shelves were lined with jars of specimen samples of . . . something.

There was a small desk on the right-hand side of the room, of such a tacky build that I couldn't help but be reminded of the shitty build-it-yourself quality furniture on the ground floor; and there was a familiar gun placed on top of the desk. In the centre of the room, there was a hospital bed and an array of medical equipment that I can't quite name connected to the *thing* that lay on top of it. It was hastily placed there, almost as if someone had left it there in a hurry.

Yes, the being lying on the bed happened to be something that could only be described as a crude imitation of a human, with such a grotesquely deformed face that I found it difficult to locate even the most basic of features such as the being's nose or mouth. Its face seemed to have melted like ice cream when you place ice cream near a house fire. Severe burn marks had scorched the edge of its face . . . as if its face had been literally set alight.

For the most part, its body contained many of the same appendages as a human body. But its arms and legs were missing from the trunk of the body, and it didn't take a genius to figure out that they had been cut off to prevent this creature from escaping or acting out. Sitting on a shelf nearby were a set of jars containing dismembered body parts that may have been arms and legs once belonging to the thing on the table.

It was only after two or so minutes of staring vacantly at the creature before I realised that, to my shock and horror, this individual was still alive by the bare minimum standards of the word. Its mismatched eyes trained themselves onto us, perhaps in some attempt to convey the terrible pain and despair of its condition. The being's skin had been peeled off in flaps and spread widely over the bed, *nailed* there, maybe in a sick attempt to study this entity's anatomy. As a result, we were given an in-depth look of its internal composition. And that was absolutely not creepy and disturbing at all. Excuse me for not describing what its internal organs looked like—or the lack of them, that is, as the only identifiable internal organ inside the poor creature appeared to be something resembling a gigantic, still-beating purplish heart in the centre its chest cavity. On top of the organ lay a discoloured hazy eye with layers of mucus and slime encrusted on it. Multitudes of sinewy tentacles of flesh that seemed to be able to move by its own free will were directly connected to the heart.

Yeah, sorry, but I don't think I can describe its internal organs any further, as I cannot describe the rest of the organs within the creature's body with my limited medical knowledge. Furthermore, I'm afraid that I might puke out the contents of my stomach should I dwell upon that ghastly image any further, and I'm sure you don't want that, do you? Yeah, I thought so.

Even with it being so horrendously mutilated, it was still not dead—as I said. Quite a miracle, I must say, and that was precisely why the creature looked so haunting to me. Imagine if you were at a funeral for a car crash victim and the deceased just sat up and started screaming while ejecting bile and vomit? Yeah, I don't think you would be able to get that image out of your mind ever should you actually be unfortunate enough to witness what I just described. If you feel nauseated and somewhat disturbed, magnify that feeling by roughly a hundred and you will have a fairly accurate understanding of how I felt back then.

But no, that wasn't even the first thing I saw when I walked in there. The unfortunate elephant in the room happened to be Albest, standing directly on top of the gurney, holding what appeared to be a gigantic black dildo that he was about to bring down on that guy's heart. He froze mid-action and, the, uh, 'tip' was left dangling a few centimetres from the hazy eye in the middle of the creature's exposed heart.

The atmosphere in the room was so awkward and thick that you couldn't cut through it with a chainsaw.

It was as if the universe itself froze on its tracks while we drank in the situation and Albest attempted to find an explanation—*any* explanation—that could somehow justify the scene unfolding in front of us without making it look like . . . well, that. Needless to say, he failed.

"This isn't what it looks like," he sputtered, uttering the most awkward and clichéd sentence to have ever be conceived by writers since 'come here, you are gonna want to see this' out of context. Anywhere else, and especially rom-coms, that would be a hilarious one-liner warmly received by a diverse audience of canned laughter and pre-recorded applause. Not here.

Especially not here.

"Albest. Is this . . . a sex thing?" I asked.

He hung limply, like that of a puppet with its strings cut. He looked like he was stuck between feeling a combination of embarrassment, constipation, awkwardness, and unwelcome surprise, and trying to find the off switch for his emotions. I'm sure he tried to look emotionless, but he failed. Like, really hard. His face might as well have turned into an open book, but even that would have said way less than the emotions flashing across his face at that moment. It essentially said, 'oh man, what I would not give to be literally anywhere else doing literally anything else right now'.

"No!" he said. "No, it's not. I swear."

His facial muscles twitched rapidly, and he stared at the dildo in his hands as if seeing it for the first time, yelped, and then flung it to the opposite side of the wall and attempted to make eye contact with Jane, who was making the difficult decision of deciding between judging him like a pile of excrement or averting eye contact altogether. A microsecond passed, and she decided on the latter, making a sharp left turn and inspecting the mould on the wall, which happened to have formed itself into the shape of Australia. I was pretty certain that she could give less of a damn about the pattern made by fungal mould, but she had suddenly decided to take a rapt interest in it as though she was staring at an original copy of Jane Austin's *Pride and Prejudice*.

"Jane, listen to me. I can explain," Albest said, hitting the cliché bingo with the prodigious speed of a seasoned idiot. "That wasn't a dildo!

I was simply trying nail a tinglethub into his ploobasilicouschleemschlackle!"

"Right. I'm so glad we clarified that it was not a sex thing," Jane drawled out in sarcasm, stretching out the "i" sound two seconds longer than it needed to be.

"I swear, what I am doing right now is an entirely normal surgical operation," Albest explained, inexplicably adapting a patronising tone halfway through his sentence. Oh boy, he was not going to impress anyone with such a condescending tone.

"Just, uh, you might want to tell that to the police and the medical professionals." I said, looking at the scene with trepidation. "I mean, this look like the live BDSM enactment of an amputee fetish, you know?"

He choked. "Um, I, uh, don't have an amputee fetish. And, uh, I'm not doing any kinky stuff. I swear this makes more sense with context."

"And also, shouldn't there be, oh I don't know, a dramatic reunion here where you tearfully enquire after what I was forced to go through in the period of time where I was involuntarily held prisoner against my will?" he complained, stepping away from the gurney.

"Well, that was our original plan," Wu Er started.

"But you kinda undercut it with the whole dil—tinglethub insertion thing."

"Right. Right," Albest said sheepishly, rubbing the back of his head.

". . . Well, I wasn't expecting that," I joked, lightly, observing his reaction. "So, care to give us the abridged version of what shit went down?"

He coughed slightly, before gently patting the small patch of clean flesh on the thing's, uh, face. "Sorry buddy, it won't take long."

"The alarm from earlier, do you know what that was?" Albest asked, waiting for one of us to react. Unfortunately, he didn't get the reactions he wanted, and his face dropped slightly. "Well, that was the alarm for alerting the whole facility to the fact that Cell X-0004 suffered a containment breach. No, no, you don't get to say, 'no shit, Sherlock', yet. I'm still doing my exposition. You don't wanna interrupt the guy delivering exposition. Okay, so the cells with the lowest serial numbers are the most dangerous cells; these cells are the whole reason this facility was created. Everything was built around these contained objects and creatures. Most of the staff here are specialised personnel trained to do the sole job of trying to keep those things in check and make sure that they aren't escaping or getting rescued by the aliens. You see Buddy over there? Yeah, he's one of the aliens, and he was essentially being held prisoner here to be endlessly experimented on. I found him a few weeks ago when the Resistance placed me in charge of doing night shift security here. After about, let's see . . . four visits fishing for secrets and attempts to get this guy out, they found me. I got captured, and then they tortured me for a few days before I managed to escape and then you guys found me in the process of inserting a tinglethub into his ploobasilicouschleemschlackle. There's another part of the story that's up to Jane to tell you, so yeah. Your turn."

"Albest, we are going to have another totally unrelated discussion after we get the fuck out of this facility, you understand?" Jane stared at him, waiting for him to respond.

"Jeez. Yeah. Yeah. I-I-I, uh, w-will do that. Yep. Yep," he stuttered, making it one of those rare moments where Albest gets actively flustered about something.

"Right. So I've been, like, really curious about the stuff that the Resistance has been doing here since the get-go. A few days ago, I received an email containing some financial records of what the Resistance spent all their money on last month . . . and it was not pretty,"

Jane said, looking at Albest. "So I had an argument with Albest over this stuff, and then he just ... off and disappeared. I was worried sick with no clue as to where to start. Then I met up with Peter and Wu Er at the party and compared notes before going here to check on traces of where you could be. Instead we found this place, a prison hidden away from the eyes of even some of their most trusted employees." Her eyes flickered over to Wu Er as she said this.

Wu Er shook his head, remaining silent.

"So what dented the door?" I asked. "I mean, I was under the impression that you *don't* have super strength, so pardon me if I didn't know the answer to that one."

Albest turned his head back and jabbed his finger towards Buddy, the creature lying on the gurney. "He did. Before I messed up and got jailed alongside him, he was perfectly fine and still had access to all of his appendages and he wasn't causing too much trouble for the Resistance, so they left him. But, well, he thought he would attempt to return the favour, and he tried to rescue *me*. The other way around. He pushed his body to the limits when he decided to go up against the steel door. The end result was arms and legs fractured in so many pieces that the doctors decided that simply amputating him into an organ sack would be less troublesome than trying to keep him in one piece. So yeah, that would be the reason why I'm helping him right about now and not running off."

"Well, that was surprisingly considerate of you," Jane said, slightly more impressed. "Kindness goes a long way."

Albest looked kind of embarrassed and downtrodden. "Can't really say that about me, though; I'm too selfish to be kind. If it wasn't for me, he would still have limbs and he might have still been able to escape on his own. Now if you don't mind, turn your heads. The following surgical procedure has not been approved by any scientific board of ethics and is not, in fact, terribly scientific. So unless you want to see more blood and guts and unidentifiable gore, I would recommend y'all turn your heads and face the wall for a second. We are pushing for a M rating, not becoming the spiritual successor of Human Centipede 2. So, look away."

The familiar shit-eating grin resurfaced on his face. Jane shook her head as a near-imperceptible smile crept over her own face, and she turned around to face the door.

The being made a small movement with its head, either a nod or a shake.

Wu Er and I turned around, and soon, sounds came from behind me with loud and audible clarity. It took all my will to not turn around and puke in revulsion, as the sounds that I heard could only be described as "crushed raspberries."

"Oh, and here's to sweets dreams and restful nights." I thought sardonically.

Some time passed, and when we turned back to face Albest, he was almost done putting Buddy's skin back on with a staple gun. Not that this stopped me from dry heaving at the gross sight, but I *did* notice that Albest had followed the right PPE procedures and was wearing a pair of bloodstained nitrile gloves and protective coveralls whilst operating the medical equipment. I wondered briefly where he had gotten the equipment, and then I remembered where we were.

The alien was looking much better, but it still looked like a rotting emaciated corpse with fungus growing out of it. So, either amateur surgical practises were much more underrated than I thought, or the alien had an enhanced healing speed comparable to that of Wolverine. I figured it must have been the latter, considering Albest never received a higher education beyond high school, and Wolverine was also cooler.

"Well, we can't carry this guy out, that's for sure," Albest said. "I don't have a stretcher on standby and I wouldn't even have a single clue where to take him. I don't really feel like I want to lie to him about it— Oh my, what is that strange felting I'm experiencing? Is this pity? Ugh, it sure doesn't have a good mouthfeel."

"Holy shit! You're capable of pity? I thought assholes aren't capable of that!" I gasped in sarcastic shock. In all the years that I'd known him, I had literally never seen him look like this. Albest was, according to all definitions of the word, an asshole. He hated dealing with children, and he also fed my cat mouldy bread and expired food from his fridge at one point in my high school days (the result was diarrhoea like you've never seen before; and yes, I was the one who had to clean it up. He really was an irredeemable psychopath).

Albest looked at me with an expression of exaggerated shock as he replied with an equal level of sarcasm-fu, "Oh my god! In other news, the sky is blue. Thank you for telling me the obvious. Of course I can feel pity. I feel the greatest pity, man. I am so empathetic that I'll make your head spin."

Jane and I chuckled, and suddenly things didn't feel all that bad anymore. After we'd had our little laugh, we turned our attention back to the deformed thing lying on the makeshift hospital bed. "So, any ideas what do we do with Mr. Frankenstein's Monster over there?" I asked. "Come on, there has to be something we can do, right?"

Albest looked at me with a complex expression. "Well, actually there are a few things that we could do. The first thing we could do to ease his pain is actually the easiest step, seeing how our buddy over here is still conscious and appears to be in serious pain . . . Uh, I don't know. Maybe we could give him some anaesthetic drugs? Not a permanent fix, but definitely one that I feel like we could live with. I think I saw some on the shelves nearby."

Albest paused for a moment; whether it was to take a breath, or purely for dramatic tension, I don't know. But after being seemingly satisfied with our reactions, he continued. "The final option is actually my favourite, because it involves contacting your so-called 'mysterious messenger' and throwing this problem to him/her! Then it is officially none of our business! Which would be great! Jane, you brought your phone, right?"

"Uh, yeah?"

"Great! Email your mysterious messenger and tell him to track your phone. Then give the phone to Buddy over there, and they'll get him out. The aliens already have men stationed all over the city and they've had a two-month period to prepare, so they should be able to get him out quickly."

Jane hesitated, before fiddling with her phone's keyboard for a minute or so, and then tossing the phone to Buddy. She turned to Albest. "I'm trusting your crazy plan to work."

"Sure. You can trust me. I'm Albest Dor, after all. Hey, the words rhymed," he said, wriggling his eyebrows, as he flashed his pearly whites at her. Jane giggled.

I looked dubiously at the vials of pain-killers that Albest had gathered. "Are you sure we need so much pain-killers? I'm no doctor, but I am relatively certain that you've got enough there to kill a small elephant."

Albest snorted derisively. "Please, the guy looks like he needs all the pain-killers on Earth. Besides, if getting your limbs chopped off and then systematically dissected doesn't kill you . . . do you honestly think a few wee lil' doses of painkillers will do the trick? I don't know about you, but I don't think so."

"Good point," I said, shrugging.

I walked towards the horribly mutilated being. "Hey, uh, sorry for not being able to rescue you. Really, that's the weirdest apology I've made in my life so far, but hey, who's keeping track? But we would also like to get out of this place alive. Hopefully your friends or employer or whatever relationship you have with those other guys, will come along and either rescue you or . . . help you out. But let's not dwell on that, shall we? Well, have a nice day!"

I try to be nice, I really do. I don't think I'm a bad person, and I did feel somewhat obligated to help out as a well-educated mentally healthy individual of the twenty-first century. As long as helping others does not ultimately conflict with my moral integrity or affect my personal wellbeing, then I guess I can try and do some helpful things to an extent.

We left the room in a more brooding mood than when we entered, mostly because of the fact that we had seen some really messed-up stuff, and also because we were still trapped in this fucking place and I think I'd be speaking for all of us by saying that we really didn't want to be there any longer than we had to. I needed some peace and quiet to process everything that had happened. Being hopelessly lost inside a dangerous building was not making me feel any better. But hey, at least we were finally unburdened and free to leave.

Wu Er was on his phone. There was something vaguely wrong with that, but I couldn't quite put my finger on it. He was probably just playing Pong or something. No big deal. Forcing myself to not focus on the issue, I walked on.

The lights flickered as we walked down the hallway, and I caught sight of a few posters of a corporate psychiatrist advising their employees to take counselling and anti-depressant medication. Man, life was hard. Who could ever possibly have known that, even when you're slowly being brainwashed by a cult-like organisation who have about as much kindness inside them as Disneyland, you could develop depression and other fun mental disorders? I was starting to have trouble deciding who the bad guys were. The aliens blew up my house and were likely to threaten the lives of my family members, oh, and also seemed to have pissed off my friends at one point. But their opposition (who I may have become enslaved by) appeared to be just as much of a douchebag as they were, what with the cheerfully happy posters that all seemed to imply that the mental states of the people who works here are feeling the exact opposite and the whole unethical deal with keeping prisoners thing going on for them.

"Huh, what an interesting poster," Albest remarked casually, clearly not giving quite as much of a damn as I did about the poster, much to my disappointment.

"I think there might be a deeper story behind

that poster," I said to Albest softly. A slight sense of paranoia had started settling in after spending so long running around, avoiding guards and various other security measures while the containment breach siren gradually indicated to us that our window of escape was shrinking. My insides churned like they were on a rollercoaster from a slight excess of alcohol. I felt like a lab rat trapped in a maze that I couldn't solve while anonymous scientists stared down at me in the background. Every footstep made me feel naked and exposed with every single secret that I'd ever held being revealed.

"It is still a poster, though," Albest said.

The longer we walked, the more and more things felt . . . off. Wu Er was leading us now, walking with a confident gait. I should've felt safe. Everything should be over. We got Albest, we had all the information we needed, and we'd tipped off the aliens.

So why did I feel like I was being held at gunpoint?

"Hey, uh, Wu Er?" Albest said. "Do you know where you're going?"

There was something wrong with his expression. Like a deer caught in the headlights of a car, suddenly unsure of what to do next.

"Of course I do," he snapped. "I'm leading you to the safe exit. Not far from here, just another . . . Yep, we're there." He stopped in front of a bright yellow door marked SEWAGE DWASPOSAL UNIT #1 in Comic Sans. "Here it is. We escape through the sewage disposal unit; it should lead us right out. Don't mind the typo, there was a printing error with the manufacturer. I promise that it's also one-hundred-percent soundproof inside as well. No one will be able to hear a peep."

"That's strange. Didn't you just say you had no idea where we were going a while back?" Jane said. "I distinctly remember you being as surprised as the rest of us regarding the existence of the secret prison here. Yet suddenly, you've turned into a veritable expert on the layout of this entire facility. Mr. Wang, what's going on?"

"I didn't lie to you," Wu Er said with frantic pace. "It's not my fault. Not really. I was being really honest. This is the *'sewage' disposal unit,* and it's not like you guys were forced to follow me, at all. This would've happened anyway."

My stomach sunk as the realisation of what he was talking about pierced through. The phone . . . He was on his phone on the elevator. Something scared him. Then he started distancing himself from us. He was fiddling with his phone again after we found Albest, and he went on to lead us with such a confident swagger despite the fact that he couldn't possibly have known where any of the exits were. Not without . . . someone telling him.

"I'm sorry," Wu Er said. "But my job . . . that comes first." With that, he pressed a switch near the door. A trapdoor swung open about two steps behind us. Unfortunately, movies had led me to believe that trapdoors opened directly under your feet, so I reflexively leapt backwards directly into the pit of darkness that came up to greet me.

Everyone else did the same.

I should've watched less Wile E. Coyote as a kid, I thought as the cold unforgiving darkness enveloped us, dragging us into what might very possibly be a murder basement.

I hoped it was not as soundproof as Wu Er claimed.

13

I WOKE UP WITH A SPLITTING HEADACHE THAT COULD
only be described as 'What it must feel like to be
hit by a car and then forced to listen to it spout
cold jokes that fall flatter than a punctured hot air
balloon'.

Sorry, that wasn't what it felt like. That was the
psychedelic head-fuckery that I experienced while
unconscious. *Some asshole* must've drugged me. I
crinkled my eyebrows in annoyance. God, it felt like
trying to move my body through Jell-O. Though, I
was tied-up with heavy rope on a rotating carousel
possibly appropriated from an abandoned theme
park.

I let out a heavy breath. "This is some *Saw*-level bullshit. What is he, a hack?"

Well, at least this answered a few questions. Now I was one-hundred percent sure that Wu Er was a double-crossing asshole.

"So, you're awake already, eh, Pete?" Albest chuckled sluggishly, looking at me with what appeared to be a friendly smile. "Sorry, I know this looks bad, but I swear we'll get out alive."

I looked around. There were three people beside me. They didn't bother to gag us; looks like they weren't too concerned with us making too much noise. It made sense; no one ever checked the sewage units to see if there were haunted ghosts inside. Just ask Pennywise. The jerky movements and the creaky hinges told me that the whole damned thing was a jury-rigged contraption that wouldn't pass construction codes even with a hefty bribe. Heck, this thing was probably decommissioned before I was even born. As someone who worked in product design and presentation, I can tell you with some certainty that most amusement parks wouldn't use this model anymore; the risk of ejection was too high as there were no safety straps or railings to prevent rider injuries, ropes and physical restraints tying us to the ride. *The Resistance probably bought this off a junkyard or something,* I thought. Funny what the mind will do in order to distract you from the threat at hand. The rust and the flaking paint on this death trap indicated aging of at least a few years out in the environment.

Despite the mass of design-related information flooding my brain as I inspected the ride, I failed to notice the stranger in our midst struggling against his bonds until he started shouting. "LET ME GO DAMMIT! I HAVE NOTHING TO DO WITH THESE LITTLE MAGGOTS, well, except for training and observing them for over two months and exchanging several off-the-record conversations with them over that very period. And I was also the person responsible for handling their relevant security clearances in case of a security breach, BUT WHO'S COUNTING ANYWAY? I'M TOTALLY INNOCENT, LET ME GO!!"

I flinched at the familiar voice. "Steve, is that you?"

"NO, IT IS THEODORA FROM ACCOUNTING— OF COURSE IT'S ME, YOU IMBECILLIC SHIT. YOU MAGGOTS DRAGGED ME INTO THIS!"

"Steve, I know you're an insufferable asshole," Albest said, "and we haven't really gotten the chance to connect with you enough, but I'm sorry that you've been dragged into this." My personal opinion was that Albest long ago lost the right call anyone else an insufferable asshole.

"DAMN RIGHT YOU SHOULD BE. I WAS CUDDLING WITH MY DATE IN BED, WATCHING A HORROR MOVIE RIGHT WHEN SOME FUCKERS KICKED IN THE DOOR AND DRAGGED ME KICKING AND SCREAMING OUTSIDE!" Steve shouted, leading me to the uncomfortable realisation that Steve had no indoor voice. He needed no megaphone or voice amplifier to make himself heard.

"Um, so, is that why you're naked and strapped to an amusement park ride with what looks like a kilogram's worth of lube slathered liberally on your body?" Albest asked.

"YES, I was very, very, sexually aroused at that moment. She was just getting out the whip and dumping the whole bottle of—"

"Stop. I'm going to stop you right there," I said. "Too much information." Let's just say, I was pretty damn grateful that I couldn't see his body.

"Can you wriggle out of the bonds with how . . . wet you are right now, Steve?" Albeset asked. "Also, I really want to wash my eyes with bleach right about now."

"Well, they got a bondage expert on hand when I was, ahem, arrested," Steve said, "So, even if I could, it would take a while. Also, you see how much rust is on this shit? I don't wanna get tetanus. Wriggling out might mean contracting some exotic disease."

"Steve, you are literally our only hope right now," Albest said. "This is a situation where the better choice is literally the risk of contracting something dangerous, and the other option is dying at the hands of a torture device so devoid of creativity and ingenuity that it's essentially an intellectual property theft. Trust me, I've been there. The good folks burning the midnight oil at ER won't question why a grown man covered in lube and cuts was being admitted there."

It was at this point that Jane finally stopped pretending to be asleep and started shouting in shock. "You what?! Jeez, Albest, we *really* need to have a talk."

"Yes, yes, sure. But now's really not the time to explain. Besides, everyone has had an uncomfortable sexual encounter before, right?"

"Nah. I'd reckon I was a good judge of character," Jane said, pausing for a moment before she immediately retracted her previous statement. "Actually, that was how I thought of myself before I met you. But it's still a no. we really do need to have a talk."

"What about you, Peter?" Albest said, shocked and slightly offended at the jab at his character.

"Hey man, is this some sort backhanded insult? You know you could summarise the entirety of my sex life on a post-it note. Don't rub salt into the wound. You know that my personality is so fucking bland that I can't hold a girl beyond the second date. The last time I tried to start a relationship, my date confused me for a packet of oatmeal cereal! Like, how does that even happen? Neither my first name nor my surname has, at any point in time, been Bran. I mean, she could've confused me with the kid from *Game of Thrones*, but I fail to see any similarities . . . so I'm assuming that she was thinking of the cereal."

Albest giggled, and then so did everyone else.

I cringed. "Guys, on a less depressing note, we are all about to die. So, uh, please stop laughing at my sex life, or the lack thereof, like it was the funniest punchline that you've ever heard."

"Hey, sorry man, didn't mean to. I just kinda forgot the fact that you have a track record of really messing up relationships just by being genuine. But in all seriousness, you probably need to have a more vibrant personality in order to look interesting enough to date, and I mean the good kind of interesting. You do not want to be me while dating, you just gotta trust me on that one."

"Yeah, don't worry, I understand. So, is there any way out of this place?" As soon as my voice left my mouth, an old television set flickered to life, as if it was pre-recorded, which was also pretty damned bullshit. You can't really make an old telly do something like that because old TVs don't have pre-record functions . . . so maybe the damned thing was retrofitted with a timer or some shit. Whatever, I needed to take my mind off the fact that I was about to die, and the TV seemed a good distraction.

"Hello, hello, hellooooo . . . I am your executioner." Wu Er's fat wrinkly face appeared onscreen, draining horror out of the situation faster than getting fired from *The Apprentice*. Personally, I thought the jigsaw killer did it better. *"Hey, uh, sorry about double crossing you guys, but I assure you, it was nothing personal. I'm just doing my job, and well, it's going to look very good on my resume if I managed to weed out the sleeper agents planted into our organisation by the aliens. Hm, what's that? Was anyone saying 'oh but we aren't sleeper agents planted by the aliens'? Well, it doesn't matter, you aided and abetted a prisoner who was a known operative loyal to extra-terrestrial forces, and broke*

several codes of conduct when you broke into areas that you have no security clearance to access. You also performed an unauthorised injection of anaesthesia into prisoners, and operated a HICKLER—again, without authorisation. Oh, this certainly looks like a bad track record, doesn't it?"

"SAY IT TO OUR FACES YOU FUCKING COWARD!" Steve screamed, or maybe he had just managed to find his voice again after temporarily losing it from excessive shouting. He struggled against the bonds as wet, slapping noises resounded against a metallic surface. Now, you will have to excuse me, as I was positioned three seats away from where Steve was and didn't exactly have a clear line of sight of what he was doing. Whatever it was, it was presumably something gratuitously offensive and probably involved flopping against the restraining cotton rope bonds and handcuffs. I knew that Steve escaping his bonds would be the best chance of us escaping this situation alive, but I somehow failed to feel even one iota of excitement when I realised that I would essentially be rescued by a naked drill instructor from hell who happened to have very weird predilections in bed.

Naturally, Wu Er couldn't hear what we were saying, and the camera zoomed out. Revealing that

Wu Er was standing in Warren's office with the big man himself and Jeremy looming behind him, their faces an unreadable mask of apathy.

Wu Er grinned. *"Now look at me. I'm about to be promoted by Warren himself and I get to rub it into Jeremy's face while I'm at it! Finally, I will never need to search through another file again and I will finally have the security clearance to oversee everything. Warren promised, oh yes he did. I can just see the jealousy on your faces right now. You poor pathetic people leading meaningless lives, I'm about to become a Senior Domestic Field Nourishment Engineer—wait, what does that job title mean again?"*

It took me less than two seconds to translate that job title into plain English, as my lifelong experience of decoding corporate double-speak and obfuscating job titles finally paid off. My panic and anger were almost immediately replaced by bemusement as I watched Wu Er proudly point at himself and brag about his imminent "promotion." Oh, it was quite a promotion alright. Wu Er shrugged and continued his monologue.

"Alright, so you know the drill. Now's the part where the torture device gets to work and everything will be recorded for us to review at a later date. Fun, eh?" He stared at the camera, cackling, making nausea-

inducing sounds in his throat. I'm going to be honest here, the man sounded like a dying hyena having sex with a dumpster. Yes, it was that bad. Always practise your laughter before becoming the evil antagonist, it's all about the presentation. People wont take a cackling idiot seriously, for example.

Albest looked nonchalant. "You know, I've been threatened with a violent death so many times now that I would frankly feel more emotions if you just straight-up offered me a painless death, Wu Er. But it's not like you can hear me anyway. Oh well. I came here with the assumption that I'd be brutally murdered; you're not exactly breaking new ground."

The drama on the screen unfolded. Warren opened a box containing a neat little badge that he pinned onto Wu Er's chest. He patted Wu Er on the shoulder, and gave a little smile. *"Congratulations, you are now a Senior Domestic Field Nourishment Engineer,"* he said. *"Good luck on your journey."*

"Huh? What do you mean, boss?" Confusion came over Wu Er's face for a brief instant as he finally deciphered what being a Field Nourishment Engineer meant in very literal terms. *"Oh god, no! NO! PLEASEIDONTWANTTOD—"*

BANG!

Jeremy fired the gun, expressionless as he watched

Wu Er's body slump lifelessly onto the ground. Warren shrugged. His figure flickered on the screen as everything fell out of focus. *"Toss him into the field, the plants needed the fertiliser during days like these."*

On that note, Jeremy dragged the corpse out of the room, leaving only a trail of blood behind as evidence of the crime. Warren dusted imaginary dirt off his immaculate suit, and walked towards the camera to turn it off. It was only then that I managed to get a closer look at Warren's physical state.

Warren didn't seem to be doing so well. With bloodshot eyes and grey skin indicative of seriously deteriorating physical health, he coughed, and then he turned off the camera with an arm that was riddled with needle marks and bruises. I can say with a reasonable degree of certainty that whatever he was shooting into his system, it was not antibiotics and paracetamols. A trail of what looked like a mixture of spittle and blood was making its way down the corner of his mouth as he leaned in to turn off the TV. The image held for two seconds more than I would've preferred to linger upon the image, and then it went blank.

The spinning carousel abruptly came to a screeching halt at the same moment the TV stopped broadcasting the tape, and then split apart as miniature railway tracks clicked into place, sending the four of us in four different directions towards four very uncreative death traps that must have been designed on a tightly controlled budget.

My seat quickly detached and was set down onto a railway track towards certain death. I'd reckon the whole place here was built on about a hundredth of the research and development budget required to create a working prototype of a homicidal murderbot disguised as a vacuum cleaner. Priorities, man. These people need to sort out their priorities.

Albest seemed to be completely unfazed by everything that was happening around us and seemed to be . . . fidgeting his thumbs? You'll have excuse me, I was busy being sent towards destination fucked; I wasn't really paying that much attention to what everyone else was doing.

Screaming, I'd reckon.

There was something at the far end of the room, which vaguely resembled the skeleton of an electric chair. Obviously, this exoskeleton was meant to be attached to the seats of the carousel. The cruellest part of this elaborate design was that the damned ride chugged along the rails at the breakneck pace of . . . slightly faster than walking. I don't know about you but screaming for ten minutes just to be executed in the most pathetic way possible feels like the punchline of a cruel joke. It was like this entire murder dungeon was designed by a sadist.

To add insult to injury, even after the seats mechanically clicked into place with the hovering array of wires and electrical conductors, it only set off an agonisingly slow Rube-Goldberg machine powered by pneumatic pressure pumps and a confusing series of spring-lock hinges and dynamic motion propellers hot-glued onto the wall. In short, this was the nightmarish murder basement of someone who appeared to have failed every single mechanical engineering course in all of existence, masturbated to *Saw* religiously, and then decided to prove his worth as an engineer by building a down-sized version of something that would arguably impressive and horrifying . . . had it worked in the way it was supposed to. So . . . basically the *Saw* equivalent Human Centipede 2 but with none of the awful parts. Being awful does not equate to being a visionary, I swear, if our imminent death is being shot by black-and-white cameras . . . I'm going to be so pissed.

As someone who worked so, *so* intimately with designs, I could spot about three different design flaws in this that would've been obvious to anyone who bothered to actually spend the time and effort to think the torture plan through.

Perhaps the most important flaw here was that the rails didn't align perfectly due to an inaccurate measurement. So, in theory, if I tipped my entire body weight in one direction, it should cause the ride to capsize and I could just slide free.

But first, the hard part of the whole scheme: waiting.

Remember what I said about this damned thing being so slow that it would barely outpace a toddler? Well, yeah, the misaligned rail tracks were at least another forty seconds away from me. If I could time my movement of action correctly, I wouldn't need to be rescued and I could easily struggle free on my own.

I waited.

Twenty seconds to go. The skewed lines were only barely visible in front of me now. The timing needed to be absolutely perfect, or else the ride would just rock and continue on down the tracks.

Fifteen seconds to go. I started feeling cold from my shoulders down as self-doubt welled up within me. Could I do this? Would I be able to do something? I froze. My body wouldn't respond, and I knew that it was partially due to the panic and fear, but I was also relatively certain that it was because whatever those bastards pumped into my system was not mixing well with the alcohol that was still in my body.

Ten seconds. I tried moving my legs to no avail. Shaking it, imploring feeling to come back, I pushed, and I imagined my legs flexing and moving again. But they did not. I had to force myself to stay calm and keep my heartbeat down. Concentrate on the goal at hand. Focus on stay alive. One two, one two.

Five seconds. I couldn't see the skewed portion anymore. From this point onwards, I was relying on pure instinct to guide me to survival. As soon as I felt a bump jolt the carriage, I was going to lean as far right as my body would allow me to.

I felt the bump before I heard it, and with a yell, I shoved myself to the right, crashing into the side of the machine. My shoulder smashed into the metal coverings. The pain was bad, but it was suddenly so very worth it as I felt the car tip, its centre of gravity shifting right, jamming the wheels on the track, stopping dead, and finally capsizing.

Hitting the ground with a familiar crash, I tasted blood. I was no longer on the tracks, but I was lying dangerously close to a segment of exposed wiring shooting out little arcs of electricity. Every second inside this sewage disposal unit was a game of the engineering equivalent of Russian Roulette. If the electrical discharge touched any of the other devices, I could totally see how quickly this entire building would go up in flames alongside it, or if it flew into any exposed fluids. If this place actually connected to the sewers or a real sewage disposal unit, then dangerous sparks of electrical currents could light 'em like a Christmas tree.

Shaking myself, I quickly freed myself from the bonds and was only stuck with the handcuffs on. "Guys," I shouted to no one in particular. "This place has a lot of exposed wiring. Staying here for too long is *not* going to be healthy."

"Yeah, thanks for— AAAAHHHH!!!!" Steve screamed. He had slipped out of his bonds and landed on a piece of exposed wiring. It was then that I wondered just how conductive lube was.

As I watched Steve's lifeless corpse slowly collapse before me, I learned that it was very conductive. A wave of regret washed over me. I was the last person he talked to, and I had been dismissive and basically ignored his existence the entire time. This was my fault. And I hoped to dear god that there's no slo-mo cam anywhere near this cam, that would've been insulting and unappealing on so many levels.

I don't know how long I stared at his dead body for, but I do know that it was long enough for the sounds of footsteps to start echoing in the distance. "Oh dear god, they're coming."

I don't remember enough of what happened next. It was as if a haze had fallen over my mind and covered it to the point where I lost control of my body entirely. I don't know how I even managed to shuffle along with Albest. Things fogged up, and I couldn't really say I felt much of anything. No joy of escaping, no elation, no sadness, no anguish. I felt like I had temporarily become a robot as a black cloud in my heart made everything seemed so . . . distant. I didn't care about the consequences of not escaping anymore. That thing that motivated me, that drove me, seemed to be fizzling out. In the process of being extinguished.

First, we were betrayed by a close associate for a promotion inside a cutthroat organisation run by a dangerous homicidal maniac. Then, a guy we collectively hated was dragged into something that he should've had nothing to do with and died in front of our eyes. Steve was an *asshole*. I remembered the first two months of his training as some of the worst days of my life. But he was also not involved with anything that had directly happened to us. He had a life outside of the Resistance. He had a sense of humour, and he might have been the last person that I knew we could trust. He died because he stepped on a fucking *wire*, dead like a light. No epic gun fight, no heroic sacrifice. Why did they have to die like this?

We waded through a sewage tunnel that Albest found on the other side of the basement wall by using a series of mechanical tools on a nearby workbench to smash open the entrance. Wu Er was apparently so confident of our imminent death that he placed our stuff right beside us. Was he that happy about our imminent death that he would put all of our stuff right on the table? Something felt off about that, and I wasn't exactly sure what.

Their deaths thundered in the back of my head as Albest ranted about his reunion with his gun named Chekovs, which was nice. He couldn't believe his luck that it "just happened to be on the work bench." There was a post-it note beside it that had a middle finger scrawled on it with a sharpie.

Finally, I regained my grasp on reality and vomited into the sea of liquid sewage as some time passed. I don't quite know why. I trudged behind Albest, who was having a difficult time fighting rats and stomping on cockroaches while also trying to attempt small talk with Jane. I watched expressionlessly as he, unsurprisingly, botched his attempt at starting casual conversation with her. There's a time and place for everything, and maintaining a casual conversation in the middle of a sewer is simply not going to happen when the person in question is pinching their nose like a vice, and is trying their best to pretend that the brown chunks of unidentifiable objects are just mud.

We moved forward in relative silence as the skittering of tiny insects, rats, and other bugs filled the background with the exact opposite of ambient noise. Again, there's just something so incredibly nauseating about sharing space with creatures that are probably more toxic than the average KKK member, who happen to be the human-sized STDs in their own right. I, personally, have an irrational fear of insects and nasty little critters crawling over me, and just by being in close proximity with them scars me more than modern horror movies. Barring a few exceptions, of course. I remembered the cockroach I encountered back at Albest's house, which happened only two months ago, yet it felt like years. And yes, I have vivid recollections of my encounters with bugs. They're disgusting critters that imprint themselves right into my memories. Fight me.

We wandered aimlessly for a while before finally finding, to our collective relief, a manhole cover and a relatively clean ladder leading up to it that didn't look covered in shit. Albest volunteered to be the one to check where this manhole cover opened to, since nobody else wanted to climb out of the sewer only to find themselves in the middle of a highway. Doing something like that was a pretty good way of getting yourself killed.

After a few minutes of him pressing his head against it to listen for any noises that sounded extremely mechanical and car-related, he climbed down and said, "Yep. It's safe. I couldn't hear anything besides the sounds of kids giggling, vague snippets of random conversations, and the sounds of couples breaking up over adultery claims. So, I'd say the manhole cover above us is connected to a park. Who wants to be the first one up?" He clapped his hands to gather our attention and then immediately proceeded to wipe them on his clothes as he realised that he probably now had shit on his fingers from touching a dirty sewerage ladder.

With as much subtlety as we could logically muster, we climbed up from the sewer and were greeted with the sight of screaming children as they subsequently ran away from the smelly sewer-people that appeared before them. I sighed, before asking whether anyone had a credit card. To my surprise, Albest found a credit card inside 'his' wallet. Fortunately, it did not smell like shit, and it didn't belong to him. Which was good. Because it would probably be pretty damn difficult to convince a cashier to take our personal credit card, and this would also make tracking us through our credit card history more difficult for the Resistance.

We shuffled out of the park, trying our best to avoid as many people as possible, since that's a pretty good way of embarrassing yourself and a sure-fire way of causing a commotion. It was bad enough that we'd just escaped from a serial killer's misguided attempt to brutally kill us. But being detained by the police was not on the list of things that I wanted to do for the day (well, technically it was nearly the morning of the next day already, so I wouldn't know whether it would be metaphorically correct). I doubt it would be on high on anyone's to-do list.

Looking back, I heard the distant booming sound of an industrial explosion. Following the trail of smoke, it's easy to distinguish that at least something had exploded. No prizes on guessing precisely what, that should be obvious at this point.

The cashier wrinkled his nose as he gingerly accepted our credit card and gave us a reasonably grand hotel room with two complementary sets of bathroom products. It seemed like even they couldn't stand the smell of three people who had recently wandered through a sewer. Naturally, we thanked him and hoped that we would have at least three hours' worth of spare time before they caught up to us.

My phone rang. It was Warren and, hesitant to take the call, I looked around to see what the others were doing. Jane took a quick shower that was over in less than five minutes, then went to a clothing store, bought us fresh clothes, and dumped the ones that smelled like dead fish on a hot summer day in the trash. Albest was curled up in a foetal position at the other end of the room. Everyone was occupied and probably didn't have the time to offer me advice on whether I should take the phone call or not . . . so I decided to take the phone call.

"PETER, y-you sack o-o-of shit!" Warren screamed. Jeez, somehow he managed to get spittle on me from the other side of the phone line. I winced as I subconsciously wiped my face before realising that it was dry. Ragged breathing came over the phone. Well, it was either that or a very angry printer that had three different sized pieces of paper jammed in its mouth.

"Alright, simmer down," I said. "You sound like an angry blender. Noisy and also pretty damned annoying, you know?" I was trying my best not to sound nervous. "Besides, why are you calling? In case you missed the memo, YOU JUST TRIED TO KILL US! I don't think I have an obligation to listen to someone who just attempted to kill me. Also, you killed two of my friends. Are you tracing this phone call? If you are, I swear to god—"

"Peter, Peter, Peter. I'm n-not tracing your call. H-h-h-how ridiculous. I simply wanted to tell you that . . . you are welcome to come back anytime you want. B-besides, when you are talking to a guy like me, you can trust me when I say it was nothing personal. You saw Mr. Wang. He was a backstabbing thief, and he rightfully outlived his usefulness. We have everything you could ever want here! A happy, carefree life. Isn't that what you want? You and your family can live happily ever after in nobodygivesafuckville, away from all the hustle and bustle of fighting major conspiracies or being the cannon fodder of a secret war. Doesn't that sound great? All you need to do is to keep talking. Don't hang up the phone. Don't tell your friends. A beautiful life awaits you." For a moment, I hesitated, forced to choose between my friends and my future. I wanted peace and quiet so much. I wanted to abandon everything. Truly.

I looked one last time at Albest, and then at Jane obsessively sorting the clothing by colour, size, and by manufacturer on the bed. She was barely holding it together and Albest had retreated into some mental cocoon. And suddenly, I knew what my answer was.

"You know that I'll hang up, right?" I said, in annoyance.

"But you didn't," he replied, with a slight hint of delirium in his voice. God, I hated talking to this guy. It was like talking to a mentally retarded Joker. I mean, knowing the DC Universe, I was also certain that something along that line had already happened in-canon or in an otherworld series. Heh. There's some meta-humour for the whole family to enjoy.

I hung up immediately. I think it was obvious that Warren planned to trace my calls to where we were hiding, but he needed time in order to do that, and I was not going to give him what he wanted.

I sat next to Albert, hesitated for a while, before saying, "So, I want to tell you something. Do you want to hear it?"

"Is it important?" Albert mumbled, some light coming back into his eyes. He glanced at his watch repetitively, as if doing so would somehow make time go by quicker.

"Are matters of life and death important?" I retorted, grabbing a glass of water.

Albert tilted his head, looking at me with a curious

expression. "Of course they are. What, did someone go up to you and offer some grand price in order for you betray us?"

I nearly choked on a mouthful of water as Albest finished talking. Coughing, I said in surprise, "How the fuck did you know?"

"Dude. We've been friends for years. If I still haven't figured out what kind of person you are by now, I would be a terrible friend, wouldn't I? Look, from the perspective of others, you are the weakest link in the group; that's why the aliens targeted you, and that's also why the Resistance, I'm guessing, targeted you. You aren't special, and that, ironically, makes you special when you are stuck with a group of extraordinary people like me and Jane." He puffed up his chest in pride as he literally just made it all about himself.

"You do realise that you just made my problems all about you, right?"

"Well, I don't imagine you would care." Albest shrugged. "But you get the point, right? Tell me more."

I paused, grabbing out my phone and scrolling through a list of circuses and amusement parks that had closed down during the last two decades due to a gross violation of construction codes and an unethical lack safety procedures to properly minimalize rider risks. "Warren called me. He wanted to trace the phone call to our hotel room." I didn't elaborate.

Albest nodded sagely. "Yeah, well, I can tell. Oh, and it looks like we need to run."

"Huh?" I followed his line of sight towards the windows looking down the hotel's main entrance.

Before I realised what was going, a wide array of cars, vans, and motorcycles surrounded the hotel. Albest groaned and muttered something about being fucked over again by terrible luck, before grabbing his stuff and then shouting to everyone, "Alright, we're surrounded. Let's go."

"Wait, you knew this would happen?" I said, looking at Albest, who didn't seem in the least bit surprised about the sudden turn of events.

"Yeah well, the guy just attempted to kill us. Do you honestly think he would make a special exception just for you? 'Course not. He gave you the illusion of a choice and kept you on the phone long enough to trace our approximate location, Peter. You gotta think." Albest casually pulled out a few bottles filled with . . . something, and then lit the lid on fire with a lighter. He tossed them out the window and explosions quickly followed as the bottles bounced one after the other into the gathering of vans.

I turned to Albest with shock and little bit of

horror. "Albest, you killed people. Holy shit, you caused an explosion. Fuck." With trembling hands, I shook him. "Do you understand the gravity of your actions? That was an actual act of terrorism. The reason that I've gone along with your stupid bullshit is because we aren't terrorists. I followed you because I don't want to die, and to somehow shake off these stupid terrorism charges. I wanted safety. I want us to be the good guys. Then you pull a stunt like this! What do you want me to think?"

As a guy not known for passively taking blows, naturally, Albest punched back. *Hard*. I dry-heaved and Jane pulled us apart before the fight could escalate any further.

Shit. No. Now was not the time for this. It would only take them a while to regroup and, as much as Albert's ruthless course of action disgusted me, a part of me had to agree that this bought us some valuable time to escape.

"What would you have done?" Albest hollered, tears flowing down his eyes. "What do you want me to do, asshole? They were going to come after us, and they have a pretty high chance of *killing* us! What, do you suggest that we don't retaliate, and just keep on running forever? This can't go on forever, Peter, and unless you have another plan, we'd better hit them where it hurts. Fuck, dude, this shit sucks." He stared at me with an intensity that I never thought he was capable of. Clearly, the events of the past few hours had pushed him a little too far.

Albest climbed off the ground and ignored me. He started fishing around the cupboards. "Good. Now, I'm going to set up a few . . . surprises for them. I think there's a bottle of drain cleaners hidden in the back of the cabinet below the bathroom sink behind the towels and condoms. Oh yeah, and a bowl of some sort. That's perfect. You two, please leave; I'll catch up with you in a sec." He was running left and right collecting cleaning materials from the bathroom and chucking them inside a giant container. He then proceeded to dump a few bottles of acidic liquids in for good measure, before throwing in a long tie that dangled over the edge onto the carpet to make— Oh god, was he trying to turn the entire goddamned hotel room into an explosive? Look, I'm no chemistry expert, but I'm pretty sure he was trying to make a chemical bomb Rube-Goldberg-style. Seriously, why does everyone want to rip off *Saw* these days?

I furrowed my brows in disapproval. I wanted to ask him what the hell was he doing building a chemical bomb, but something inside me held me back. Perhaps it was partly because we had literally just gotten into a fight about what he was doing, and partly because I had no other alternatives to offer. Then . . . there was also a part of me that wanted to see shit blow up. So instead, I decided to step out of the room with Jane.

"You don't like this, do you?" Jane muttered to me as we stealthily made our way towards the fire exit at the other end of the corridor. The emergency maps said that this fire exit should open out at the southern end of the building at an intersection. If we moved quickly, we had a chance of escaping.

"No. I don't," I whispered. "I . . . I feel awful right now."

Jane sighed. "You know, life has a funny way of making idiots out of smart people. Not that I'm implying either of us are smart people, but hey, everything sucks. I don't think I'm okay. A part of me wants to scream and run around like a headless chicken.

"Honestly, there have been a few times when I've questioned whether there's even a point to what we're doing," she said. "I mean, the world goes on with or without us. The aliens don't seem to be doing all that terrible of a job ruling the world, considering we haven't already collapsed into a post-apocalyptic wasteland of murder and kinky BDSM-mask-wearing-perverts driving over-exaggerated muscle cars."

On that note, we opened the fire exit doors and ran down the corridor in silence. The two of us had few thoughts in our heads that we'd rather not share with each other. Albest quickly re-joined our group, and gave a confident nod of the head to indicate his existence.

Luckily, the southern exit was not crowded with the people from the Resistance, and we were able to escape with little difficulty. There were a handful of guards in the middle of the intersection, rerouting cars down another road so that they could storm the hotel without any random bystanders getting too involved. I was pretty sure it was just a drug raid or something on the local news. Good for them. Bad for us, though, because we had to sneak past them.

"I've got to hand it to them," Jane said, speaking for the first time in a while. "It's impressive how they managed to organise a raid like this in such a short period of time. It's barely been an hour since our escape from the creepy *Saw*-inspired murder basement. How do we get past them? There are a few on patrol."

Albest smiled reassuringly at us. "Don't worry.

I'll take care of them in short order. It'll be as easy as rolling a nat 20. Trust me."

That was, um, a terrible analogy, because it was . . . absolutely not reassuring at all. Albest was pretty damned unlucky most of the time; I mean, just how damned unlucky do you have to be in order to be swept from one murderous conspiracy to the next? Besides, he was terrible at making attack rolls during combat rounds from what I remembered of the RPG sessions that we shared anyways. What was he even getting at? I stared at Albest speechlessly.

"Hey, I'm not a writer," he said. "Don't expect me to come up with good analogies on the fly." He snuck towards the guard. Normally, this was the part where the hero saves the day by being epic, either knocking out the bad guys or just going Rambo on them and taking out every single individual within the area thanks to plot armour or some bullshit.

Unfortunately, that was not quite how things went.

Albest tried to sneak up on the guard, and failed rather spectacularly as the guard spotted him immediately about thirty seconds before Albest could even attempt to initiate a combat round. It was so comical that it almost felt like Albest had foreshadowed his own failure.

The guard struck first, taking Albest by surprise (oh, the irony) and attempted to knock Albest out with the butt of his gun. Albest managed to squat underneath it in the nick of time, grappling for the gun in the guard's hand.

He failed. Which was kind of expected when you stupidly attempt to grab the one thing that you can basically guarantee the opponent won't get the chance to use. Albest took another brutal blow to the stomach, which stunned him, opening him up for a barrage of punches.

Jane gave me a light shove as I snuck up on the guard and delivered a clean chop to his neck. He made a high-pitched gurgling sound, before I silenced it by jabbing him in the throat. A split second later, Albest was on the other side of him and his foot was in the guy's dick, and then it all became a bloody two-on-one beatdown. It was one way to make a ham sandwich.

Perhaps it was unrealistic to hope that the fight wouldn't attract any attention. But even though we did our business cautiously and managed to avoid making too many unnecessary noises, we still managed to attract attention onto our tail.

"Hey! They're there!" A voice screamed.

It was too much, and we ran off. We couldn't fight back against that many people. We were running for a good ten minutes without stopping to take a moment to breathe. The sound of motors flaring in the distance was all too loud. I couldn't stand it. *We* couldn't stand it.

Panting from exhaustion, I said, "What are we really going to do?"

Albest responded with only grim silence as an empty felting of dread rose up within me. "Everything's going to shit," I told him. "Where's the other side? Aren't the aliens trying to raid these guys right now? God dammit, they're still on our tail."

"I don't know," Albest said. "Let's stay behind for a while longer and check."

He stopped for breath.

"What the fuck are you doing? We can't stop here." Jane said, panicked. "There's a bus stop a few dozen metres away from here. We can't stop here."

Albest stared up at the sky in resignation. "You know, this can't go on forever. It was fun at first, I'll admit that. Maybe there's something wrong with me for enjoying it, but I liked the thrill of fighting an all-powerful organisation that was more powerful than I ever could possibly hope to be." I listened to him in silence. "I never felt in control of my life, Peter. My parents died when I was in high school, and I wasn't prepared that. My exam scores fell downwards, and then it was all downhill from there."

Oh geez, now he's started to monologue. Is the situation getting that bad? I heard the thump of helicopters approaching, yes, it seems to be that bad.

"I was unemployed and way underqualified for the high-paying jobs because of my lack of a university diploma. I survived by working odd jobs and trained for a while as a Private Investigator once I realised that it didn't require any prerequisite university degree that I couldn't pay for, and everything could be completed via online courses. The rush of adrenaline and control I felt when I cracked my first case was . . . both exhilarating and relieving at the same time. I felt I had regained control over my life and, more importantly, control over my own actions. I really felt like I could mould and sculpt my destiny into something greater . . . That was why I more or less literally pounced onto a case like this when it came across my table. It was everything I could ever look for. Hahahaha." The laugh was hollow. His words are hurried now, as if he wanted to get everything off his chest before he dies.

"I've gone down the deep end, huh," he continued. "Two years ago, killing people—whether they deserved it or not—would never be something I would even *consider*, much less do. But today, I just casually tossed Molotov cocktails out of the window onto cars and people, rigged a hotel room into a deadly chemical explosive and left all of my values behind . . . to save our respective asses. We could've saved him, that guy. I . . . I don't think Wu Er told them about Buddy, or else they would've threatened us with him already, right?"

He was breathing rapidly, and I was relatively sure that he was suffering a mental breakdown right in front of me. Unsure of what to do, I gave him a hug. "It's alright, Albest. There's still time to make things right. Do you know what we're going to do?"

Mental health problems are sometimes portrayed as attractively edgy on TV but, more often than not, a mental breakdown is pretty damned unattractive. Albest hung onto me as if he was drunk and could barely walk. I knew he was sober, unlike me.

He stayed like this for a few seconds before slowly, but surely, pulling himself back together. He caught his breath. The despair and hollowed emotions of forced apathy gradually vanished from his eyes. "I know a guy in China," he said. "He earns a good amount of money selling antiques and then reselling them. He's a fencer, but I know him from a few years back; and he owes me a favour. Once this is over, maybe we can go hide out in China or Ukraine for a while. Ukraine has lax laws when it comes to identifications. Live off the grid for a while and, who knows? Maybe we can wait it out or even start another life. Anyways, call this number and tell him my name, everything will turn out okay." A hint of determination had crept back into voice and, for a moment, I saw the briefest glimpse of the shadow of the guy he once was. He still needed a shave, though, and he look like a murder hobo. He scribbled down something on a scrap of paper, and rattled on, "Well, you guys can anyways. Those assholes will catch up to us in short order, I'll hold them off, you guys, hided there. You see that garbage dump? That's your best hope. I divert them away, don't make a single peep. And everything will turn out okay."

"I'm going to *try*," he said, "even if it's too late, dammit. I don't know whether it's possible to get everything to turn out alright, but that's what I'm going to try and do. If we have to choose between a bunch of crazy cunts trying to kill us and the aliens, then we'll have to choose the lesser evil. It's going to be a long shot, but it is definitely not impossible. Oh, and Peter, throw your damn phone away. Jane can buy you a new one later."

"Goddamit, Albest, are you crazy? You can't just

up and leave for a suicide mission at a time like this." I pleaded, ignoring the distant sounds of footsteps and yelling, and with tears streaming down my face, "Come on, let's just get away all this already."

Jane was crying behind me, but she didn't move.

"Peter, those guys have cars and motorcycles. Unless you and Jane have some sort of superpower of outrunning cars and motorcycles on foot, I'm your best shot at delaying them for at least another ten minutes. That should give you guys enough time to make it count, right?"

He grinned. "Don't just stand there, *hide*. I'll go off and give 'em hell for long enough to make it count. I'll make everything better. Trust me."

And he ran off.

Bewildered, we hid within the trash pile, sobbing and wrecked, with our new clothing already stained with smell of garbage, sweat, and blood. And we waited for the noises to dim. We waited for the footsteps to go away.

Shouting.

Then a rapid series of gunshots.

Silence.

This truly is the darkest timeline.

14

FINALLY, THERE WAS PEACE AND QUIET. OR SOME semblance of it, anyways.

We'd managed to reach a motel. A cheap one, like the kind where people OD on drugs to commit suicide. They don't ask questions and they don't give a shit about who's renting their rooms. As long as you can give them money and you aren't carrying a dead body, they'll let you stay for at least one night without getting nosy. It was a significant downgrade from the semi-luxurious hotel that we were staying in just thirty minutes ago, but it was in the farthest reaches of the cityscape and it was safe. That said, this place could not have been more depressing if it was placed right beside a graveyard. At which point, they should just change their slogan to "hey, it was your choice, man; don't ask us why you did it."

The only good thing about this place was its anonymity and the fact that it only had three floors—which would make escape in the worst-case scenario much, much easier. I have to say, it was tense. Nobody felt like talking after what we'd just been through. Once adrenaline wore off, it became a pretty damned stressful night. Jane had gone channel-surfing the moment she found out that there was a TV in the room. She was hoping that there's some piece of information that could tell us whether Albest, that fucking idiotic asshole, is safe. Back then, that was the only thing that really mattered.

Jane had it worse than basically anyone else. I mean, she had to deal with Albest (a full-time job all on its own), nearly got killed, translate elvish, got betrayed by a trusted ally, got trapped, watched someone die (again), and didn't even get more than fifteen minutes worth of peace and quiet before having to run for her life again. As if that wasn't enough, she also had to cope with Albest's nervous breakdown and took his stupid decision on stride (personally, I think it was just because Jane had been too numb at that moment to really process what had happened), she helped us find a place to stay so we didn't have to sleep on the streets; and she single-handedly managed to convince the cashier to give us a discounted rate for our room, as well as the WI-FI Password, *and* a twenty-five percent off coupon for a neighbouring pizza shop. Jane was practically carrying the whole crew forward.

I was eating a small slice of Hawaiian pizza that Jane purchased. To be honest, I was sure Albest would feel disappointed if he realised that he would be missing out on the chance of eating some Hawaiian Pizza. After all, a pizza was a pizza, and not being held captive seemed like enough of a blessing as it was. We'd bought the pizza with a twenty-five percent off discount coupon, which meant it tasted roughly twenty-five percent better.

"Welcome to Incredible News, afternoon edition! I'm your trusty news reader John Journalist!" the man said, looking directly at his teleprompter to the left of the camera. *"Joining me today is my partner Anne Anchorwoman! How do you do, fellow human-people, we too, would like to assure you from the desks of Incredible News that, as fellow human-people, we feel just as devastated by the latest terror attack on one of the most prominent administrative offices within the city. Rumour has it that it has affected the local sewage*

system as well! Prime real estate gone to the S-H-I-T, wouldn't you say, Anne Anchorwoman?"

"Yes," Anne said, reading from the newscast with a picture-perfect smile. *"John, I think we should also consider the death and injuries sustained by the other humans in this tragic incident?"*

A stock of a burning building was shown with the accompanying text: 'Due to a copyright issue, we cannot actually show you the image of the burning building, to replace it, here is the image of an equally-devastating terrorist disaster that is not-at-all the equivalent to the event'.

"Well, Anne, I think this is terrible news, what with millions of estimated deaths and trillions of injured in that building," Anne said robotically, looking at the camera with an empty gaze and forced a smile. *"But the good news is that we have obtained an exclusive interview with one of perpetrators that are now in custody! To protect his identity, his face will be censored with a mosaic and his voice will be altered."*

Jane and I gasped in surprise for a moment, as our attention focused on the screen. Sure enough, Albest showed up.

Well, technically, his face was censored and he is wearing sunglasses, but the censors had chosen to rather oddly leave the sunglasses as-is, leaving it the only clean patch of uncensored content on Albest's face, and of course he is wearing Willy-Wonka sunglasses just to drive home the point that he is doing fine and are still an asshole.

"*Wow, F*▮▮▮▮*, nice to see you all are d*▮▮▮▮ *a*▮▮▮▮ *being all fine and d*▮▮▮▮*. A*▮▮▮▮*, funny how it all ends up, eh?*" Albest cursed in bleeps, giving the censors a hard time to scrub the words clean. "*I would like to say a few words to my fellow associates before we begin the interview: Pressure* ▮▮▮▮ *and* ▮▮▮▮▮▮▮▮*, the real asshole and tell him that* ▮▮▮▮ *and they'll show proof that—*"

The screen abruptly cut back to the news anchors, dumb-founded and insensate, they looked like they fired a circuit board trying to figure out how to spin this angle. After an entire minute of uninterrupted silence, Anne Anchorwoman finally regained her smile and said, "*Well, and that concludes our interview with the perpetrator, he had indeed offered fascinating insight and now we'll cover the news of a farmer who is making a killing selling steaming piles of bullshit and let us all focus on the farmer. Live from somewhere else, unelated to this mess, let's hear it from our friend in the field, John Journalist!*"

"*Hi! Dear viewers, you must be surprised, why, I'm sure you're expecting someone else standing in front of an actual field doing an interview with an actual farmer, but it is, in fact, actually me, John Journalist standing in front of a green screen faking it very authentically.*" He smiled, baring his teeth.

Jane shrugged indifferently.

Finally, Jane said, breathing out a sigh of relief, "Well, we can deal. It's okay; it's not the worst thing that's happened thus far."

"So," I asked Jane solemnly, "You feel any better? It seems like at least Albest is alive and kicking and making everyone uncomfortable about what they can and cannot show on network TV. One of the most common and over-done tropes used in movies these days are back-stabbings. It's not going to give your character depth and the only thing it does is make it look like a cheap lovechild between M. Night Shyamalan and Quentin Tarantino films—the bad ones." Somehow, my attempt at consoling Jane turned into an awfully specific complaint aimed at the film industry.

Jane laughed. "Peter, how do you *really* plan on rescuing our buddy, exactly?"

"To be frank, I have no idea," I said. "You can't possibly expect me to be awesome enough to draft up a three-stage plan of action with fall-backs and fail-safes all within a few minutes. But hey, at least we have one advantage: they don't know what we know."

Taking a deep breath as I tried to subdue my rising panic, I said, with a slightly shaky voice, "We going to do this as quickly as possible. Even under the assumption that they don't find us here and that he is somehow miraculously rescued right under our nose, we still don't have enough time to draft up a coherent plan for escape, Jane. We need to end this here. They aren't going to wait, and the next time we call in with a negotiation between us and the Resistance, that's probably going to be the last time we're going to hold anything resembling a negotiation with the Resistance."

Albest nodded in agreement.

"So what are we going to exchange with the Resistance in exchange for his life? We can't go there empty-handed. We'd be walking straight into a death trap with no clear guarantee that it's gonna go smoothly." I flipped out a notebook and began drafting up a rough copy of our goals and plan of action. There was not much, but it was a start. Within moments, a rough map and a one-page list of things to do was drafted up.

"What about the information we have on the Resistance already?" Jane said. "I mean, I stole a few documents from them beforehand, I was put in charge of organising their data, remember? We can trade info for Albest, and, if worst comes to worst, we do have contact with the Aliens, we could offer that up as a last resort. I reckon they might be eager enough to kill us for information like those."

"Do you have them with you?" I asked, excitement in my voice. This could be our ace. Only . . . "Wait, if you have sensitive information on the Resistance, why didn't you bother to share it with us before? That would've been kinda useful."

"No, no it wouldn't. There was no opportunity for us to bargain back then, and I lost the copies of the documents. What I have on them is in my head, and even if I managed to recreate what I remember verbatim, it wouldn't be enough. Besides, that would only give them more reasons to kill us since we would lose any value to live in their eyes."

The back and forth exchange went on for another few minutes or so as we nailed down the details of our plan, which included how to not get killed as an accidental by-product of stupidity. So naturally, it took some time for our plan to emerge in its full form, and I have to say it was a terrible plan that we came up with.

The plan was atrociously simple and there were

not an awful lot of things we could do to change it. The very fact that we were up against a monstrosity of an organisation armed with nothing except a few guns, our wits, and an utter lack of shame wasn't exactly comforting.

Any and all shameless tricks and pragmatic strategies would be used simply to compensate our unfortunate inadequacy when compared to the Resistance: an organisation so big that, even now, we haven't figured out precisely how big or small the damned thing was. Was it the size of a terrorist cell? Was it the size of a Fortune 500 company? Or was it the size of a country, with operatives in every inch of the globe, waiting to strike at the perfect opportunity? Don't try to plot against unimaginably powerful entities at home, kids.

I could barely sleep that night, filled with so much damned nervous energy. But, luckily, we managed to get through the night without any unwanted interruptions of any sort.

Though, now that I look back on it, I might have been more scared of the morning.

15

BY THE TIME I WOKE UP, JANE HAD ALREADY returned with groceries and had whipped up some decent food for our breakfast that was *definitely* more nutritious than pizza. I spent the better part of thirty minutes tearing my guts out on the toilet almost immediately after I woke up. It was definitely not something I would want to experience again. You would have thought I learned my lesson on eating pizzas of questionable quality after living so long in a dinky town where most of the so-called "restaurants" are basically money laundering fronts for the street gangs and politicians with ambiguous sets of morals. They weren't exactly known for high standards when it came to employing cooks and buying ingredients for the shit they serve, you know? But after such a long time running away from crazy assassins and being hunted down and nearly killed, some of my 'common sense' was lost. I guess I just couldn't give enough of a shit last night and I had chose pizza over starving myself.

Jane was a brilliant cook. I've got to hand it to her. In less than ten minutes, she transformed raw ingredients into a deliciously nutritious meal complete with a relatively salty bowl of soup that satisfied my weak stomachs.

Turns out her secret was to keep it light and balanced, not using any meat (since meat takes longer to prepare than vegetables), crisp veggies that are easy to cut and prepare, and to use spices and toppings sparingly, not excessively. Nothing that will give a sugar rush either.

After her segment of "Jane's cooking advice" was over, Jane went out to buy the necessary items in order to execute our little plan. After ten minutes of nervously waiting for her to return, she came back with a tiny shopping bag. And so we began our plan with me being nominated to execute the first part after three rounds of paper-scissors-rock. I don't think it was hard to guess how that went.

Begrudgingly, after a moment of hesitation, I picked up one of the burner phones Jane bought for me last night, making good on her promise to get me a new phone on the condition I throw away the old one, and called Warren. That's right. The first damn step of our plan was to call the very guy that wanted to kill us. Still think this was a good plan? Think again.

Now was not the time for lofty goals or any bygone dreams of denial. Now was the time to put our plan into action.

With a serious expression on my face, I focused on the dial tone of the phone. One wrong step could mean death for all of us, and yet we had somehow arrived at the unanimous decision that I was to be the one to negotiate with the crazy guy. Seriously, I was not fit for this job, but Jane was . . . well . . . Jane refused to talk with Warren and insisted that a white-collar worker who had experience in Customer Service and had a brief stint working at the Resistance's call centre would have a higher chance of success than a librarian who had spent the better part of last year not being a librarian.

"'Ello? Wh-who's c-calling?" This was it. I made an inaudible gulp as Warren's voice came through over the phone. His slurred voice was capable of inducing a great deal of stress within me. I hated this irrational feeling of fear, anger, and stress that seemed to bubble up within me whenever I hear this annoying guy's voice. I felt like I was an overcooked version of Gordon Ramsay; I didn't necessarily like feeling like an overcooked version of Gordon Ramsay. Nevertheless, I did not hang up the phone and struggled to contain myself as I tried to strike a diplomatic conversation.

"Warren. This is me, Peter Stewart," I said through gritted teeth. Despite how it looks, I feel like I should explain that I hate talking to assholes—even though Albest admittedly has a few flaws himself. But at least Albest is capable being a good person when he feels like it. Warren, on the other hand . . .

"Ah? It is you! Peter!" he responded with an exaggerated happiness, an octave too high to truly feel genuine—which was actually a pretty goddamned accurate understanding of Warren's character, I guess. With some annoyance, I held the phone away from my stinging eardrums. Bad cell-phone speakers generally emulate high-pitched voices in a way that I feel was almost intentionally designed to make the user feel uncomfortable. The combination of bad reception and low-quality mics can often result in an unholy sound that will make your dog's ears bleed. Okay, it wasn't that bad; it was *worse.* "I see you've changed to a different phone!" he said. "How absolutely wonderful! I'll have to work my staff to *death* trying to get your latest locations now. A-and here I tho-thought you'd met an unfortunate fate with clowns when your last registered location was a storm drain!"

"Well, yes, Warren, it is me," I calmly said. "I think you know why I'm even bothering to talk to you after you attempted to send us to our deaths. I should probably remind you that we are still alive, and no, please don't send more people after us. I must say that we are not impressed with what you tried to pull. I . . . think I might have preferred being hunted down by a crazed clown than being forced to deal with you." This was where I attempted to convert the nonsensical small talk into a negotiation of sorts, the sort that wasn't going to end with our dismembered bodies being thrown into the dumpster, obviously. "Now, you have something we want, and we wish to negotiate."

"Heeeeh? *I* sent you to your deaths? I don't remember doing that. Hehhehheh." He laughed deliriously. There were no traces of the calm and relatively composed man left inside Warren. Back when he introduced me into the Resistance, he was still, at the very least, coherent. Now, he was nothing of the sort. He resembled more a gibbering mess than someone who was supposed to be left in charge of the important stuff. We knew Warren had some position of authority within the Resistance, but how exactly had this obviously unqualified and mentally-ill idiot managed to get into a position of power? Something was off, and I couldn't quite put my finger on it. It was almost as if there was a missing piece to the puzzle that I was supposed to get, but I was too stupid to connect the dots. "Oh," Warren continued. "And about the . . . what was his name? Doesn't matter. We f-found your little friend in our midst. Ah, is that what you we-were looking for?" He stuttered and fumbled through his sentences as though his mouth was stuffed with cotton balls. It was almost always a bad sign when you were trying to negotiate with someone who didn't sound sane and you were expecting things to turn out alright.

"Alright, listen," I said seriously, trying to get Warren's attention. He knew who we wanted, and that shifted the balance of power over to him. "We have knowledge of aliens, and we have the locations of their secret headquarters that you can conveniently find. We also have a lot of information about the Resistance that I'm sure you guys would *not* like made public. The Deus-ex-Machina stuff. These juicy titbits are only a few keystrokes away from being uploaded to Wikileaks. We have an entire encrypted data file down on a USB drive. Are you sure you don't want to work something out?" Beads of sweat rolled down my forehead, grazing my eyes. Looking at the brand spanking new USB Jane bought, and the data that she had spent two minutes transferring onto the stick from a nearby internet café, I received some reassurance that we still had the ability to hammer down the terms of the negotiation.

"And why shouldn't I just k-kill *him* and then call in a raid? Why shouldn't I kill *all* of you?" It was a good question. It really was. Now, I had to bullshit my way through that. I secretly made a mental note to complain about not brainstorming more thoroughly when we wrote up the initial conversation points. Thankfully, we wrote down just enough to talk about during the phone call. As long as I didn't veer off-topic, I should be safe.

"You *could* do that," I said, "but then we'd just upload the whole thing onto the web. Right now. The release is timed to be released online, unless we are alive and around long enough to deactivate it . . . you guys will find that you have a huge scandal on your hands as your entire organisation gets lifted out of the shadows, and into the public eye. Even if every single one of us dies, I'm pretty sure you're going to be halfway up the chopping block already because we're going to expose this whole operation." This was it. This was the final moment. The moment of truth. All or nothing. I gulped as I awaited his response. I tried pretending to sound more desperate. "If we die; y'all gonna die with us. I doubt the higher-ups will much appreciate having this on your record."

There was a long pause, and some indiscernible noise, before Warren returned to the phone and said, "Oh yeah. Sure. W-we don't want, no, we don't want you doing this at all. Now, we can negotiate and work something out. Yeah?" He was acting strange, like he was just having an ordinary phone call or calling for a pizza delivery rather than trying to strike a deal with a group of people he really wanted to kill. "But, just to make double sure, what can you tell about this "dirt" that you have on us?"

"We know about your access to alien technology. I can quote an exact number for the horrific number of human experimentations that the Resistance has committed to exploit alien tech at large. That's how you created HICKLER, wasn't it? We know of an unrelated synthetic biochemical product that can give people damned near superpowers . . . except for the fact that it is extremely addictive and just about as healthy as taking more than fifty grams worth of pure, unfiltered crystal meth."

Silence. "G-go on. Tell me more."

"Yes, and apparently this product could also be used in auxiliary with lobotomies and facial-modification surgeries as it can 'program' muscle fibres and bones to bend and distort in ways that they're not supposed to. Let me ask you a question: where did you 'rescue' Jeremy?"

"An alien experimentation camp. Horrific, isn't it? The awful, awful things aliens will do to a creature that's an entirely different species to them. The things that they're willing to do in order to corrode humanity," Warren said in a tone of cold apathy. We knew the truth, and he knew it too. Yet, he didn't even bother to offer a slight deviation from it.

"I've always wondered, why would Jeremy have a tattoo of Chinese characters calling him a cockroach on his back, when he was kidnapped by aliens," I said. "Why would they tattoo their prisoners like that? Furthermore, Jeremy has clearly been tortured before. You can't possibly be implying that aliens torture their experiments for the evulz, right? Because there's only one species on this planet that I guarantee will torture another human being out of sadistic joy, and guess what, I don't think it's the aliens." A slight tremor overcame my voice as I continued to speak. I could only keep up the cool-guy act for so long. My legs were jittering. "We give you the USB and will not upload the documents on the condition that you let him go."

"Ha! Well, t-then I will text you an address. Go to that address this afternoon and we'll perform our transaction there. How's th-that sound to you?" Warren said to me with a slurred voice that gradually descended into incoherent ramblings that I couldn't quite make out.

"Sure. That sounds fine," I said curtly, and then hung up the phone. Almost immediately, I scrunched up my eyes and threw the phone onto the table. Cold sweat stained every inch of my back as I reeled in fear and shock. I couldn't believe I did that.

Oh god, the entire damned phone call was almost ninety percent pure, concentrated, undiluted bullshit that I pulled out of my ass on the spot. I mean, sure, we wrote a brief script and outline that I managed to stick to just so I didn't end up stuttering and sounding like an unconvincing liar. But, the thing is, too many things had *already* gone wrong.

The only 'evidence' that we had so far was what Jane had stumbled on over a few drinks, purely circumstantial speculation over Jeremy's origins, we connected the dots on that one a little too late; and the only 'incriminating' things that we had on hand that were related to the Resistance was a document that Jane vaguely remembered reading.

There were no elaborate tax trails nor were there any grand, elaborate plans. Our so-called initiative of rescuing Albest was founded upon a heavy layer of bullshit thought up over a night of impulsive decisions and emotional breakdowns coupled with pizza and beer, and our plan relied on Jane's memory. I mean, yeah, I trust the memory of a seasoned librarian, but we can only go so far in terms of conjecture and deduction with so little to go on. As a corporate worker, I can tell lies without sounding like I'm obviously lying, but believe me when I say that I was nervous during that stupid phone call. I was nervously worrying that, in the time that Warren took a pause, we'd be ambushed by a barrage of troopers storming down our hideout. We would be so fucked if Warren realised that I basically bullshitted my way through the negotiation. So, so fucked . . .

The USB did not contain anything incriminating either. But the files on there were encrypted with convincing metadata forged to *make the file look authentic*, whatever that meant. We just made the file correspond to the date that we arrived at the

Resistance. If they actually decrypted the file, they were going to have quite a surprise on their hands. I looked away from it, as I did not want to risk accidentally crying from how screwed we were.

Jane looked at me sympathetically as curled up into foetal position and started muttering to myself. "Peter, are you okay?" Jane asked kindly.

"No. Of fucking course not," I shot back reflexively. "I just talked with a guy who wants to kill us and dance over our graves! Somehow, I managed to broker something resembling a tentative negotiation with a madman. Do I *look* okay?"

That stopped Jane from talking, and made me feel like an asshole.

"But yeah," I said. "Thanks for your concern. I just need some time alone." I still wanted to punch someone for coming up with such a stupid and reckless plan, but then again, it wasn't like we had a lot of time to plan this whole thing out.

I took a ragged breath as I tried sort through the jumbled mess of my emotions internally. I felt like I was going to go insane if this kept up any longer— and I am not exaggerating. There's something about dealing with evil assholes and playing their twisted games of hide-and-seek that has the power to slowly drive you over the edge.

"Hey, uh, it's too late to back out of this crazy farce, isn't it," I said after an uncomfortably long moment of silence. I wrapped a kitchen knife that I found in one of the drawers of the kitchen up tightly with a piece of fabric, before placing it inside one of the inward-facing pockets on my jacket. It was not much—bringing a knife to a gun fight is always a pretty bad idea—but it was still a much better idea than going barehanded. I wanted a smoke, but I was too tired to head downstairs to buy a packet of Camels.

"Yeah, it is," Jane said, and somehow, that reassured me. We were all going to die anyway. No one wants to die, but the cold, unfeeling rules of the universe don't care about what the carbon-based monkeys feel, do they? So, might as well make the most of it and die in a cool way. Jane tossed me a packet of Camel; she must've bought them while she was out purchasing the 'props'. I smiled and took a few steps towards the door, before stopping.

"Let's go get a drink," I said. "I think I still have a hundred-dollar note on me." We were all going down together, so I figured, might as well get drunk before heading guns-a-blazin' and running headfirst towards near-certain death.

On that note, I bought a few bottles of liquor and had a depressing drinking session that was filled with either uncomfortable silence or sad stories of the biggest fuckups and regrets of our lives. Jane drank orange juice while I shared some stories with my closest friends: There's Johnny Walker, Captain Morgan, Sailor Jerry, and tJack Daniels. All my closest pals were here to motivate me. Yay.

I don't remember precisely what happened, but I'm pretty sure Jane ended up silently collapsing into a sobbing fit as she stared at a pocket knife with a contemplative stare at the end before I collapsed into a drunken blackout.

I don't even wanna know, man.

The last conscious thought I remember having involved a colourful collection of swear words targeted towards Warren and a secret hope that we would somehow survive whatever nasty surprises the afternoon would have in store for us. And reunited with Albest, that too.

16

WITH BLURRED VISION, I SCRATCHED MY HEAD AND
tried to deal with my raging headache and the ever-
growing desire to vividly regurgitate the contents of
my stomach. I managed to make it to nearest trash
can before expelling liquid vomit into the trash bags.
Groaning, I shuffled to the bathroom to clean myself
up.

After five minutes of staring at myself in the
mirror, adjusting my hair and making myself look
less like a drunk who had just crawled out of a ditch, I
got dressed and made myself looked dignified before
re-joining the civilised world.

I went downstairs and managed to convince the

attendants for the first floor to allow us to borrow a few grubby magazines to peruse for a while. I also grabbed a satchel of coffee powder and a cartridge of milk and made myself a latte, just so I could shake off that hangover faster.

"Fuck, everything is going wrong." she said with a sigh and an expression of regret. "I would have preferred *not* doing the bullshit shenanigans that we cooked up last night vis-à-vis our plan. But . . . " She trailed off, before gently dabbing her face with a few pieces of tissue. Our plan was pretty bad at that point, not really all that different from a suicide mission. But, for the sake of our sanity and Albest, I still believed we should go through with it. There's guilt, and then there's Guilt with a capital G. I wouldn't have a good night's sleep again if I didn't at least try *something* to save my best friend from the clutches those guys.

"Yeah, I understand, but there really aren't many good alternatives to choose from," I said. "After all, we're just trying our best. I don't want to think about the consequences of our actions; I just want to live an ordinary fucking life that I'm probably never going to have now." I looked at my watch; there were less than forty-five minutes to go. We needed to start getting ready.

Jane grabbed a small pocket knife and printed out

a mapped copy of the building that we were going to do the negotiation in. "You know, we never really had time do a detailed review of the meeting place, and we are probably walking into a trap; but here's a copy of the architectural plan of the building. Especially the top floors."

"Wait, you found this on the internet?" I asked incredulously, as I stared at the floor plan in my hands. I couldn't believe it; she'd saved our asses again. Maybe, just *maybe* we might have had hope. And maybe there was a chance of improvising our way out of this.

"The internet's full of wonderful things," Jane said. "You would be surprised at how easy it is to get your hands on private information there. We live in an age of digital interconnectedness, and the only thing keeping hackers from taking what they want is your stupid password. Honestly, I'm actually more shocked at the fact they didn't change their default admin passwords than the fact I managed to get anything at all. Unencrypted data files are pretty easy to get when you know what you're doing and you have a stable internet connection."

"Are you sure this isn't a trap, though? I don't understand much about computers, so forgive me if I sound like a prude, but don't you think it's almost too easy how those plans were acquired?" I said, stopping Jane dead in her tracks as she struggled to come up with a convincing rebuttal suggesting otherwise. It's an undeniable fact that the Resistance micromanages almost everything they can and they probably would've tampered with easily-accessible records at this point if they're confident enough to try and get us to that tower.

In the heat of the moment, we never really bothered to think that our little exploit might have seemed too good to be true.

With a shaky breath, Jane said, "Well, regardless of whether it's a trap, as long as we keep in mind that this is only a reference point for us to execute our plans and not something that we have to follow to the letter . . . we should be fine, right? There's got to be some truth to the floor plan, and here's a suggestion, how about we just operate under the assumption that no plan survives first contact with reality?"

"Jane, I hate to tell you this, but our plan was the literal textbook definition of failure. Just because no one's complaining, it doesn't mean every parachute on the plane is perfect."

"Point taken. Did you bring the 'props'?" she said. "I mean, it's so crazy it might just work, right? This is how the movies say it'll go . . ."

I motioned to my little duffle bag of stuff. I could only hope that we pulled it off, bluffing our whole way through. It definitely beat getting shot at and forced into hiding, I suppose. It was the logical way out of living a shitty life since, at the very least, we would have something more worthwhile to do instead of just running and hiding cowardly.

Well, here's to leaping to our death with open arms, I thought sardonically, as I hopped onto a clean and cheap rental car that Jane managed to get for us during her little 'walk'. One minute she was going for a walk, the next she was driving back a car. That told me way more about the type of person my friend was than I wanted to know.

"Get in the car, Pete," Jane said with a slightly impatient tone. "It's going to be a half-hour drive from here and I'd prefer it if we could get there as quickly as possible. Let's get this over with quick. You'll be the hostage negotiator." She attempted to start up the car. "This bloody thing set me back a good three grand for the day. Now, I officially have less money on me than the average hobo. If we get out of this alive, I'm afraid we're going to have to skimp a bit on *food*." Jane grunted on the last syllable, before finally getting the car up and running.

The car came to life as a large puff rainbow dust,

fairy glitter, and everything nice was shat out of the exhaust pipe like a beautiful waterfall of liquid-y diarrhoea. The car meowled in protest as it was rudely awakened from its gentle afternoon nap.

It was about damned time when we finally managed to reach our destination; the tiny screeches and pony music emanating from the car made me feel nervous and annoyed.

With a tired sigh, Jane nodded unpleasantly. Obviously, the journey had taken a toll on her as well. She mumbled about something incoherently, and we shuffled towards the front entrance of the building.

"Hello there," I said, walking up to the security guard with phone in hand. "I happen to have an appointment here." I pointed to the location on the phone. "Do you know how to get here?"

The security guard stared at me as if I was an idiot. After a pause, he said, "Ask the receptionist. How the hell would I know? I stand here for a few hours, and then someone else takes over my shift. It's not as if I'm a tour guide."

I stared at the guard sheepishly. I suppose it was . . . somewhat embarrassing that I'd somehow come to the conclusion that a random security guard was capable of answering all of my questions. And so, I walked into the main lobby area under the disapproving stare of the security guard with Jane trailing close behind.

The receptionists looked bored, with collective mask-like expressions of forced smiles and what appeared to be steady eye contact—but I could tell they were really playing *Candy Crush* underneath the table. The fact that they were wearing extremely reflective glasses gave it away. "Greetings, how may I help you today?" one of them asked with a professional smile, still playing *Bejewelled* underneath the desk. Don't get me started on the other one.

"Um, I'm wondering how to get here," I said, giving the receptionist my phone and showing the address texted to me from an unregistered phone number that I was assuming was owned by Warren. Suddenly, the receptionist stopped fiddling with her phone and stared at the location with an intense expression. Her face changed several times in less than a minute as she typed up something on the computer. Finally, her face settled on a pallid mask of fear. "I-it's t-h-he fourth room on the right-hand side of the fortieth floor. The highest floor."

"Thanks, miss. Have a great day," I said mildly, walking towards the stairs . . . and then backtracked and headed for the elevator as I realised that it would probably be a very bad idea to try and climb forty floors' worth of stairs.

We walked into the only elevator available at the moment. Jane tapped her wristwatch in irritation and squinted at its displays for a long time. "I think . . . we are running a minute late."

I stared at her. "Well, it doesn't really matter now, does it? We're only running a minute behind. It is really not that bad; it's just a difference of a few minutes. I mean, everyone must've had one of those moments where they go to a meeting five minutes late before, so what's the worst that could happen?"

Gunshots rang out and the sounds of glass shattering punctuated the end of my little speech. A dull scream echoed punctuated the end of my speech with an almost ironic quality to it.

"Okay," I said. "I regret saying that now. We need to run. Actually—"

"Wait," Jane said, fiddling with Albest's gun. She quickly loaded up the gun, and flicked off the safety.

"Jane, please stay outside. When I shout 'Blueberry Muffins', rush in and save me and Albest's ass in case this goes down as terribly as I think it will."

Jane held the weapon gingerly between the tips of her fingers, as Albest hurriedly explained his sudden addition to the plan.

"But—" she started.

"No buts, I'm depending on you. Thanks." There was a tiny *ding* and the elevator doors rolled open.

I ran towards the sound of the resounding gunshots.

I burst into the room, panting. Before me was a wide, abandoned room in rather shoddy condition compared to the rest of the building. It was, on the whole, very poorly maintained and contained many flawed and irregular aspects to it. At the back of the room, conveniently blocking off the fire exits, stood Warren and Jeremy.

In the centre of the room was Albest, and there was a splatter of blueish liquid trailing out from the direction of the shattered glass frames. At first, I didn't realise who it could've been that was tossed off the ledge, then I saw the medical apparatus tossed to the side like scrap metal and the look of horror on Albest's face. Then everything clicked together.

The blueish liquid was *blood*. Though likely not of the human sort.

Dark thoughts entered my brain and I stood trembling with a similar expression of horror affixed to my face as Warren stared at me with a sickly smile.

"So, you've finally decided to show up, e-eh?" he said with a disgusting falsetto and stutter. "I-I was h-honestly getting-n-g a bit sick and tired of waiting for you. The th-thing was too noisy, so I shut him up. Everything's quiet now. *Nobody will interrupt.*"

"You killed him because he was noisy?" I said in horror.

He shrugged, as if affirming what I'd said. A piece of cotton fell out of his tattered and grimy suit. He cursed, before quickly shrugging it off. "W-well, I th-th-thought you weren't coming. You brought the flash drive?"

I gritted my teeth. The USB drive was fake. It was nothing more than a shoddy prop.

Warren retrieved a black rectangular device, powered it up, and opened the palm of his hand. "I'm going to check it myself. Now, hand me the USB."

"Not until you untie Albest," I said. "Either you give back Albest, or the deal's off and we expose the Resistance to the world, for what it really is."

"Of course. Of course," Warren said. "I'm a man of r-reason, you see. Mister Stewart. One word from me, and Jeremy will free him. I call off the men stationed outside, and y'all get a three-day head start. I just to check the contents of the drive."

"So do it now. Make the phone call," I said, holding the USB threateningly, feigning the motion of being in the process of throwing it out the window.

"Fine. Fine," he said, irritably, as he fiddled with the rectangular box, which appeared to be a PDA of some sort, and held it up to his ear in an awkward position. "H-hello? Yes. Yes. All personnel on standby and hold fire to POI until further instructions. Over."

Warren hung up, and turned his attention back me, he looked apologetic. "Alright, n-now, give me the drive before Jeremy shoots you in the head. I'm done being nice for the day."

I gingerly placed the thing in Warren's hand. He grasped it in excitement and giggled with a drug-addled laugh. Plugging the drive into the black box, he pressed an icon and started browsing through the files. The file extensions were hidden and the actual data was encrypted; anything less would've blown our ruse long before it started. The stuff on the drive looked about right, and that was good enough. Warren didn't give it any more thought as the box started decrypting the files on the drive.

"Now, I ha-ha-have no more use for you," Warren said. "Jeremy, *diposhh* of t-them." He laughed maniacally as he saw the files were in the process of being decrypted. With the speed the box was working at, it would probably only take a few minutes at most.

"Wait, wait, hold on. We can talk about this," I said hurriedly, panicking. This wasn't going according plan. Hell, five minutes ago I lost track of what step of the plan we were on.

A look of exasperation and mild irritation came over Albest's eyes, as though he was silently communicating "Well, duh. What the fuck did you think was going to happen?"

Oh dear fucking God, I hate this shit. I thought, with no small amount of frustration as well. It was absolutely typical of Albest, he was about to be killed and the best he could manage was a look of mild irritation.

Warren's wretched smile widened, if that was possible, in some sick display of his triumph against us and his maniacal power. Jeremy slowly pulled out his pistol from a holster and flicked off the safety. A growing sense of dread and despair enveloped me. It was one thing to try and talk our way out of this, but it was another thing altogether to try and outrun bullets; I mean, when's the last time you managed to persuade a gun not to aim itself at you? The gun owner, perhaps, but almost certainly not the gun.

Well, Warren was still laughing when Jeremy shot him in the face.

17

JEREMY PACED THE ROOM, FOR THE FIRST TIME showing some flicker of intelligence and emotion in his impassive eyes. Warren's corpse collapsed forward, and twitched reflexively for a few moments in some awful manner before all life ultimately drained from his tortured visage. A look of incomprehension was still engraved upon his face.

He shot Albest on the shoulder, "Don't you fucking move, or I'll bust you harder than when we had our happy fun time in the lab."

Some deformed snarl of a smile flickered across Jeremy's face as he turned toward me, stamping over Warren's dead body with his feet before turning to face me. He let the silence grow deeper, making me feel about ten kilos heavier. I felt paralysed, I can't scream. "Well, I suppose you didn't see this coming now, did you?" he said.

I shook my head with all the intensity and vigour of a bobblehead-doll as, suddenly, everything added up. "So, I'm guessing you aren't as incapacitated as everyone thought you were. You were controlling Warren all this time, like a puppet?"

Jeremy snarled. "And I would've gotten away with it if you meddling b-bastards hadn't interfered at such an inconvenient time! You stole from our facility; you threatened to take away our research sample; and, to make things worse, you gave the aliens their opportunity to undo everything that I've done. Do you know how long I've been doing this? All the meticulous planning it took to manipulate that asshole into thinking I was too dumb to figure everything out? It took time to get him drugged up enough to develop an addiction, and now you come here and force me to kill the fucker!"

"Hey, we didn't force you to do anything," I protested. "You did that yourself. No one said you had to kill Warren."

Jeremy ignored me. "I planned this for an entire year, taking control of the entire cell. Every carefully orchestrated 'accident' turned into a puff of smoke. The higher-ups turned their eyes to this facility last night, and I had to . . . rush things. I didn't want to make it quick, you know? I wanted to see every bit of pain and regret on his face, watch him suffer as the lights went out inside his stupid brain. Unfortunately, increasing the dosage didn't exactly work out. That piece of shit became too delirious to control."

He took deep, rattling breaths as he stared at us. A wide grin stretched over his ghastly face as his features slowly shifted ever so slowly before becoming an exact replica of Warren's features. With a growing horror, I realised what his plan was.

Naturally, I obliged, since he had a gun. It was generally a very good idea to listen to the man holding the gun.

"Okay, okay," I said. "Whatever you say, whatever you say."

I casually glanced at the entrance before regaining some modicum of confidence.

"Now," Jeremy said. "I am going to be very polite now, and I want you to jump out the window before I shoot you—since I consider you pathetic pieces of human waste not worthy of the bullet. Then I'll kill your friend and his bitch. I want you all to *suffer*."

"Oh really? Well, BLUEBERRY MUFFINS to

you, you dirty sack of shit!" I screamed as I rushed towards Jeremy-Warren-Thing with an intensity that could only be described as *Rambo*-esque ("Sorry, is this reference too American? I can change it if you want . . . what? It's fine? Ah. Okay, then."). I managed to tackle him onto the ground before a slug of lead buried itself deeply in my left thigh. "Ahh! Fuck!"

Jane rushed in, guns-ablazing as she reflexively aimed the gun at Dead Warren before pausing for a moment. She paused. "Wait, there's two guys here, they both look exactly the same. Who am I supposed to shoot?"

"The one that isn't dead!" I shouted, as I tried to pluck the bullets out of my wounds. "Argh! Fuck, that hurts!" The bullet didn't come out, and well, I guess I'll just have to stomach the pain while beating the shit out of Warren. "Jane, what took you so long?"

Jane, now trying her best to aim her handgun at Jeremy, growled, "Well, if you actually listened to what I was about to say a few minutes ago, you would know that I don't know how to use a gun and I don't deal with stress well. Look, just forget about it, okay? Also, can you move out of the way? I'm trying to fucking aim and I think I might accidentally shoot you instead."

I dodged a punch from Jeremy and rolled on top

of him, and tried to choke him. Absent-minded, I screamed to Jane, "I was literally shot in the thigh because of that few seconds' delay! How do you think I can forget about this?"

"You two, shut up. Just shut up, you're making this worse." Jeremy-Warren-thing said in irritation, ignoring my flailing and tossing me aside. He flung me off of him as though I'm light as a feather. Flashes of light erupted within my vision as I coughed up some blood. Okay, I'm hurt.

Finally getting a clear line of sight, Jane shot That Fuckface in the knee. I think her hands was trembling, and she missed her *intended* target by at least thirty centimetres. It was too low to hit the mark.

"Look, can we just focus on the matter at h— Oh my god, Albest," Jane said, distracted by Albest, who had, rather unfortunately, fainted right when things were getting interesting. Apparently, he wasn't the kind of guy who could shrug off a bullet wound. I cursed something awful under my breath as I saw his eyes roll back into his head. Fuck, I guess we'll just have to make do with two-against-one. That can still work, right?

Jeremy stumbled back a few steps, before regaining his balance as though nothing happened. He was totally unfazed by the bullet holes in his body that . . . had hit none of the vitals. Goddammit, Jane had the aim of a stormtrooper.

"Jane, please give me the gun," I said.

"Hold on, I wanna try something first," Jane said, suddenly very excited. Holding the gun with two hands this time, she took aim and lowered her voice. "Oh, Jeremy, I'm going to kill you."

Jeremy laughed, as if amused by her threat. To be honest, Jane really was the polar opposite of intimidating. "You wouldn't dare, and even if you did, you can't even aim properly! Hah. Y-you couldn't hit me when I was standing still! Pfft, and you think a woman like you can kill me? How about this, I'm going spread myself out and stand sti—"

"OH YOU WANNA TEST ME, FUCKER? YOU WANNA TEST MY AIM? YOU KNOW I'M GOING TO USE IT, OTHERWISE THIS GUN WOULDN'T FUCKING EXIST!" Jane roared, channelling Steve and ripping several holes in Jeremy's heart, penis, and abdomen.

I completely retracted my previous statement about Jane not being intimidating. Hell hath no fury like a woman scorned.

Jeremy stumbled back up as he plucked the bullets out of the wounds, blood coagulating almost instantly. This time, though, as Jane tried to shoot him down, her gun clicked. There were no more bullets left. Her face paled.

Jeremy's fist sailed through the air, connecting with her jaw and flicking her onto the ground like a cockroach. The ground literally shook as she landed. She lay there, bleeding and coughing like Albest, obviously in no shape to do much of anything. Jeremy then shot her in the heart.

"No!" I screamed, about to rush towards Jane and Albest. I froze as I saw Jeremy aim the gun at Albest, ready to pull the trigger.

"Stop, or I kill your friend as well," he said. "Well, actually, I plan to kill them anyway. But if you move even a single step from where you are standing . . . I will kill him right now. And then I will torture you."

I stared at that scene with horror and despair, I felt helpless, and I couldn't do anything to stop it. I must've looked pretty awful in that moment, as I just saw one of my closest friends bleed out and die in front of me.

And so, that's how I ended up having a staring contest with the business end of a gun. I happened to know for a certainty that it had enough bullets inside it to not only kill me, but to miss a few times whilst doing so. I . . . don't have a lot of faith in the Jeremy's shooting skills.

For the past few weeks, I've questioned what I had done to deserve this. If there's an all-knowing God out there, it would stand to reason that I had pissed him off at some point in my life, or else none of this would've happened. If I was ever to make a list of my biggest crimes against humanity, it would probably begin with not brushing my teeth when I was ten and end with the stupid decision of reading the entire Twilight saga just to find out whether it was good or not (hint: it's a decision that I regret to this day).

Perhaps there'll a different ending in store for me instead of the usual "shot in the head and die" gimmick that tends to happen around me, I just wouldn't bet on it. I comforted myself with the knowledge that, at the very least, I wasn't stupid enough to flail my arms around, screaming and wetting my pants at the same time. Which was at least comforting enough to know that I'm still sane and I'm probably going to die thinking and doing something incredibly stupid. I . . . think I'm fine with that, I suppose.

I'm about to die unceremoniously from a bullet to the head, with my best friend gagged and hog-tied no more than five metres away from me, unconscious. My eyes flicked to Jane, lying on the ground, quite dead. It's not that it doesn't look cool or anything; in fact, I'm sure it would look great if this was a scene from a movie . . . but we happened to be on the top of a building. In real life. And I happened to be standing on the edge of said tall building with a gun pointed to my head—as I mentioned. Two of my best friends, dead or unconscious; and I'm not even given enough time to grieve.

Fuck, I don't want this.

"I want you to understand that you aren't supposed to be here," Fake-Warren said, as he theatrically waved his free hand about when he had realised that there wasn't actually an abundance of things that he could do to look more threatening. "You really would never be here if it wasn't because of your curiosity. There isn't going to be a single thing that can save you from getting shot in the head."

He stared at me, an expression of casual hatred on his face. It wasn't the face of someone who was angry; it was the face of a person who is about to squish an ant that crawled into its food.

A random paper bag flew into my face, and about sixteen different "Save Our Environment" ads and that annoying song from *The Lorax* started playing inside my head. That's right, I am not in my right mind right now.

Jeremy was monologuing, he still was. I just tuned

him out; the last thing I want to remember in my life isn't going to be that jerk's super-villain monologue.

"Hey, do-do-do y-you know how many times I had to rehearse this speech? I-I-I have a speech impediment; this took me months to perfect. If you don't at least pretend to care about this, I will—" He realised that I wasn't listening at one point.

"What? Kill me?" I said, interrupting him in mid-sentence. Residue anger boiled within me as I ranted onwards for a few moments.

His face reddened into that beautiful hue of red and purple people thought could only exist when an eggplant and a tomato had a baby. Well, the people thought wrong. "Why don't you just jump off the building then? I could just shoot you right now."

A brief exchange happened between Jeremy and I before he finally finished his speech . . . I think. He probably said something dramatic, though unfortunately I didn't realise it during that moment, as I was too consumed by rage to really care about anything else at that moment I had decided that, if I'm going to die, I'm going to go drag that piece of shit down with me.

I picked up a shard of glass, and I slammed into him, slashing all the way down from head to throat, and I half-expected a bullet to embed itself within my head.

"FUCK YOU AND THE HORSE YOU RODE IN ON!!" I screamed, my life flashed before my eyes as I decided to take the bastard down in a suicidal act of stupidity.

Jeremy never did make the shot. Perhaps he had finally shot off all the bullets within his gun, or maybe the pistol jammed (something that I imagine would not have happened if he used a superior weapon). But I still fell off the ledge of the building, and a look of gloating triumph was glued onto his face as the last expression he'll ever make. The ledge of the building quickly flashed upwards in a hazy, indistinct blur.

Falling from this height was still going to have the result being me dead on the pavement, flat as a pancake (though I would be bringing someone else down with me). You don't exactly need to know quantum physics to realise exactly how screwed you are on a scale of one to ten (hint: it was an eleven) when you're falling from a very high point on a building.

Wind whipped into me harder and harder, as I briefly pondered about my life decisions; lamented the fact I'm going to die on a Monday; and wondered whether I still have any regrets left. Well, I guess

Albest will probably be sad, but I think he'll survive. We managed to rescue Buddy. Well, technically, the aliens did it. Funny how weird that sounds without context, right? The entirety of your life becoming meaningless as death comes rushing up to meet you? Yeah, I guess Albest really was right when he said that my life was a bad joke.

Oh well, however improbable, I suppose Jane have a chance to live. I think . . . I'm okay with dying if this was how it all ends. I hope my friends survives. I hear sounds of police sirens nearby, maybe I'm mishearing, really, that could happen, and if they manage to get here on time . . . well, who knows? I just hope my sacrifice was enough to help them survive. My life would finally have meaning.

A satisfied smile came over my face as I continued my descent downwards. Suddenly, my phone rang, oh yeah, my mum and dad was still round, I have siblings, a job and oh my god. Ohshitnonononoidontwanttodi—

EPILOGUE

I WOKE UP ON A WHITE HOSPITAL BED WITH A SET
cast covering both of my legs, and an I.V. drip stuck
to my left arm. I felt like I was missing half of my back
felt and I was pretty sure about half of my skeleton
had been replaced with metal.

All in all, I was surprisingly intact for a guy
who had just fallen from a tall building. Frankly,
I wasn't expecting anything more than either the
man downstairs narrating my life-story to me
while I plunged into a pit of fire to burn for all
eternity, or being a lifeless slab of meat waiting
to be scraped off the road, or even something
along the lines of permanent paralysis with some

of my limbs missing from the impact. But I was surprisingly . . . intact.

A chrome silver wall and a middle-aged doctor stared back at me as I struggled to sit up on the unfamiliar bed. He raised an eyebrow, grunted, and then proceeded to ignore me and chose to focus on scribbling words into a clipboard as he muttered about something.

"Mr. Stewart, you're finally awake," the man said after he finished writing. "We were almost . . . worried that you wouldn't make it, especially after spending so many resources to keep you alive. Face it, you aren't Superman, and there was no way you could've survived that fall with injuries as light as this without a surgeon as *great* as me holding the knife. The state we found you in was something that most doctors and surgeons would immediately classify as 'a dead man' since most of the bones in your lower torso were fractured and you were five minutes away from meeting your maker, who I imagine would have been terribly disappointed in you. It was truly fortunate that we made it in time and managed to save your sorry little life, though you'll find reclaiming control of your legs to be a little bit difficult for a while . . . but that's to be expected, as most of the bones there weren't yours to being with and there were a few parts here and there that we were short on, so you'll feel some metallic replacements. Some of the orthoses were custom-made in less than two hours after your fall, I assure you that such things would be elsewhere."

He pursed his lips disapprovingly at me, as if he was disagreeing with the flaws in my facial structure. "Overall, there shouldn't be any serious side-effects or repercussions, since your body was operated on by a true master surgeon whose shining brilliance is years ahead of his own time. Unfortunately, no one appreciates my genius." He sighed in disappointment.

The man somehow managed to keep a poker face and a monotone voice while he shamelessly bragged about how great he was. I suppose there will always be narcissists like this no matter where you go.

He explained my new daily routine, gave me an estimate of when I would recover, and went through the diets that I would need to maintain in order to recover as quickly as possible. I quietly listened, partly because I was a quiet person by nature, but mostly because my throat was really parched and I was afraid to find out how long I'd been unconscious.

"Alright," he said. "My name is Friedrich Schulz. I've been your supervisor for the last few months or so that you've been unconscious. I don't see that changing anytime soon unless someone else comes in with all of their bones broken from falling off a tower." For a German guy, he had a surprising lack of an effeminate German accent. "Do you want some water?"

With great difficulty, I nodded.

A few hours and a quick snack later, I was on a wheelchair and could finally move my arms. The wheelchair sucked, but it came with a cup holder, which was good. Friedrich pushed me along at a slow pace. No one seemed to be in any hurry to do anything, not even the doctors. In fact, they seemed to be more interested in having small talk than revealing any grand, secret design to me. The good surgeon-man told me that I was to be escorted "for a walk." I didn't know how to react to that, so I complied.

So, after I was well-rested and feeling considerably better, I realised that my life was not in danger (at least, not right now) and I was not in a hospital. It was a strange feeling, to feel safe after such a long time inside an unfamiliar building. Maybe it was because they were the ones who saved my life, or maybe it was because of the well-preserved forest that I saw through the windows as they toured me around the complex, but I felt *better*.

I could almost say I felt . . . *good*.

They took me to a slightly different place where

Albest was sitting with his hands and legs cuffed. Jane was also there. She seemed tired and bit pale, presumably from a lack of blood, but she was at least in better shape than I was and she wasn't dead. Again, something inside me released a figurative breath of relief. We were alive. I had been dreading the absence of Jane ever since I woke up, but it was nice to see that my fears were unfounded.

"Let me go, you bastards!" Albest yelled, tugging at his restraints violently, while also loudly shouting every single swear word he knew, and quite a few more . . . creative sentences that he made up on the spot without repeating a single foul word. He would've made a seasoned sea-faring sailor proud.

I stared at the man who pushed me into the room. "Why is my friend chained up?"

"Your friend woke up a few hours before you did, and we did try to talk to him, but your friend over there has been . . . pretty uncooperative, to say the least. He attacked some of our employees here, and attempted to damage the property with a sofa and a makeshift Molotov cocktail in hand. It took us fifteen minutes to disarm him and fifteen more to find a handcuff that he couldn't break out of. He also somehow managed to clog the ground level sewage system to unleash a torrent of . . . liquid horror onto us. We are *still* cleaning that up. So we had no choice but to temporarily restrain him with duct tape and heavy chains because, well, he's pushing the edge of our patience."

"Uhh . . . I guess I should probably apologise on his behalf then," I said. "He can be a bit of a pain in the ass sometimes." Even I felt annoyed by his antics sometimes.

After Albest calmed down, the man led us all out of the room and down a long, winding corridor that seemed to lead nowhere. Being someone who recently survived a fall from a high building, I must protest that after such a long time sleeping . . . simply being guided around on a wheelchair felt tiring.

Time passed slowly as the twisting corridors became narrow, straight hallways. An almost impractically large and imposing door loomed in the distance, as if it knew it was the most important door in this entire corridor, and giving all who saw it a desire to smash it down with sledgehammers. Humans have always had a subconscious desire to either own or destroy beautiful things, especially those that have an archaic carving of an annoyingly smug sphinx protruding out of them. The stupidly confident expression on that face seemed to not only contradict the futuristic architectural style of the place, but also appeared to be wordlessly conveying the message: "I have a larger penis than you, oh and whatever I am guarding is more important and valuable than your life. Hahahaha."

The corners of my mouth twitched uncontrollably as I tried to keep a straight face staring at the incredibly realistic expression of pride and disdain on the hunk of sculpted bronze. Albest seemed to be entirely unaffected and instead was asking a pointlessly large amount of questions . . . which didn't get any answers, unsurprisingly. Not that it mattered. After everything we'd been through, it wasn't that hard to connect the dots.

The man placed his left hand on the door and a mechanical beep resounded within the corridor as the door slid opened silently, wordlessly inviting us in. I shrugged, slightly unimpressed. After all, was there even a point to resist at this point? It was obvious who we were dealing with at this point: The mysterious group of aliens that had been behind this whole mess since the very beginning. No other organisation was capable of reviving a person who had fallen from a skyscraper with nearly no side-effects and then ship said person to a building filled with technology decades ahead of its time without said person knowing it was aliens (it was me, the metaphor was referring me). Besides, it was an open secret that our mysterious messenger was someone affiliated with aliens to begin with.

A library filled with books and an antiquated fireplace was the first thing I saw, and then I saw the surveillance cameras blatantly perched on the ceiling, recording everything. A being who was obviously not human occupied the seat directly to the right of the fireplace. His face resembled the alien we had found in the Institute, with plain features that I forgot almost the instant my eyes left him. If you ask me what the colour of his eyes are or whether he had a nose, I could probably tell you, but if you were to ask me to draw his face or even describe his overall features . . . I would suddenly become incapable of describing his facial appearance.

"Mr Peter and Mr Albest, I don't believe we have met," the alien said politely, as he stood up and held out his hand-thing.

For a moment, I didn't know what to do. I mean, it was obvious that he wasn't the only alien inside this place and he certainly wasn't the first one I'd met. Furthermore, it is not only racist but also very rude to assume the worst of others when they have helped you. He probably wasn't the one who commanded the others to blow up my house, but I still felt an irrational sense of anger and injustice swell up inside me as I remembered that night. Then, I deflated and decided to wait and see how things played out.

"Well, as you know, my name is Peter, and these guys are my friends. Nice to meet you." I signalled Jane and Albest to do the talking for me since I was never very good at it. But, obviously, Albest decided to be uncooperative and decided to be an asshole.

"Alright, now that we have that out of the way, tell us what you want," Albest said harshly, sending my hopes of diplomacy off the edge of a cliff and turning the situation into a semi-interrogation. I can't say I was exactly happy with the result.

Hurriedly, I tried to smooth things over. "Well, we would really appreciate it if you could explain why you saved us and what you want from us. I'm pretty sure you wanted to kill us a few months ago, and sent assassins on our tail for that very purpose. You also framed us for crimes that we didn't commit. But now you intervened, saved my life and took us here. Why?"

The alien looked at us weirdly, pondering my words. "Very well. There's no point to any cloak-and-dagger now, so I'll gladly tell you. You had already proven to be quite a resourceful group who was recently back-stabbed by the ironically named 'resistance' that is even more hell-bent on world-domination than us. I realised we could use some more intel on the inner workings of this organisation. So, we are going to—"

"Kill us after making us suffer?" Albest interrupted annoyingly, again seemingly trying to make an already somewhat fucked-up situation even worse. I glared at him, hoping that he would get the message to shut up and stop trying to make stupid comments. It doesn't even make sense in the context of the situation.

The weird smile on the alien's face became slightly strained, as if the act of keeping a civil expression had become a terribly arduous task for him. "No, this is unfortunately not a B-grade film and most definitely is not *Independence Day*. We are going to offer you a job. It is very likely those annoying flies who very recently made an attempt on your lives will attempt something similar in the future. We need resourceful people who are capable of thinking outside the box to work under us. As the saying goes, the enemy of my enemy is my friend, and there . . . really aren't a lot of people that fulfil that criteria, so we decided to extend a job offer to you. If you decide to work for us, we can guarantee the safety of your immediate family members and a comfortable sum of cash monthly. Hell, we'll even throw in dental insurance if you want."

The being threw up his hands. "We apologise for the situation that we placed you in, but you must understand that the severe damage to our infrastructure caused by your friends really did require drastic actions to be taken in retribution, and we had assumed he had more accomplices, Mr. Stewart."

I glanced at my friends again, as Albest and Jane seemed to ponder whether to accept these offers as well. Sure, this irresponsible group of aliens tried to kill us many, many, *many* times, but it was also a somewhat logical response to the fact that Albest was an idiot who decided to overstep his boundaries way too many goddamned times. I wanted to have a normal life. I never wanted to be involved in this hotpot of conspiracy, aliens, and life-threatening situations.

Personally, I just didn't want to be fucking backstabbed by power-hungry maniacs anymore . . . but yet, I somehow did, and the chances of me returning to a quiet life of working at a normal company and living in a normal town was infinitely close to zero.

And I had braced myself for making the decision.

I sighed. "Fine, I accept your job offer. I'm still a wanted terrorist who has a stupid group of people still hunting me down for some stupid reason, but it's not like things can get any worse at this point, can it? Just show me the documents I need to sign and the procedures to go through. I want to be able to take a day-off every once in a while, and be able to work normal hours. I'm quite certain by now that nothing is going to faze me."

Albest looked at me with a weird grin on his face. "What about anal probes?"

"Uhh, yeah, no. I don't want to have some suspicious thing shoved up my ass for *any* reason." We shared a quick chuckle to lighten the mood before Jane shone a friendly smile towards me.

"Well, there you go," she said. "There *is* something that can faze you."

I shook my head in resignation and suppressed a smile. Having this kind of conversation felt like everything was back to normal and almost made me forget that I just verbally agreed to become the employee of a group alien invaders who were plotting to take over the world . . . peacefully. "Well, you know my decision," I said. "What about you guys? This time, are *you* going to be the one to follow my lead and accept the terms?"

"Wow, for the first time in forever, Peter Stewart has taken the initiative," Albest said. "I'm proud of how the shy guy who was once so average that it took our high school teachers more than three weeks to match your face to your name has finally somehow managed to not remain passive. Peter is my friend. I dragged him into this shit, and I'll follow him down the rabbit hole if only to make sure he doesn't die. Well, it's also because I feel like I might need to earn enough money to buy something that is the equivalent of a diamond ring in the near future." He glanced at Jane, who was struggling not to laugh. "I'm being serious, you know?"

"Yeah, sorry, it's just that sometimes it's a little hard to take you seriously," Jane said, chuckling. "But yeah, remember to also buy some beer. I feel like I might want to get a drink sometime in the near future. Like, a few minutes from now."

And so, as Albest and Jane shared some more friendly banter (okay, and maybe a little bit of flirting was involved, but I don't think I want to go into the details too much), we unceremoniously ended up accepting a job working for our future alien overlords.

The alien nodded sagely (or it could've just been how he looks when he's annoyed). "Well, remember to report to Human Resources tomorrow—sober, if you can. Tomorrow, the HR people will lead you deeper into the rabbit hole. And before Mr. Stewart start commenting about how stupid and clichéd this line sounds, he should do well to remember that he has said worse. And no, there are no anal probes here; we aren't in a sex dungeon, for goodness' sake. In the meantime, why don't you tell me your story? I'm sure it will be very interesting to hear it from a fresh perspective."

"Well," I narrated with mock seriousness, "the best place to start this story is probably the day after my friend 'died' . . ."

THE END

ACKNOWLEDGMENTS

AS A WRITER, I'D LIKE TO THINK THAT WRITING IS a one-man job that could be undertaken by anyone. But that's hardly the truth. There's always a team of editors, supporters, and family members behind every story cheering them on and making sure that their stories are told. Over the past few years, a lot of lovely folks had supported me and cheered me on. I owe a debit of gratitude, a hug, and at least one game of Balloon Tower Defence with the following people:

The incredibly talented, somewhat easy-going, wise, and patient Brandon Young, who was my editor. Doubtless he'll also be the one to catch at least a few grammar errors in the Acknowledgments section as well. (**He did.**) Fun fact: The book cover was also designed by him, which essentially leads me to owe him a sum of gratitude that I can't quite describe, but definitely feel.

I'd like to thank my parents, for being such lovely people and standing by the fact that their son didn't become a doctor, but chose to become a writer instead. Without my parents, I believe this book would not be in your hands in any shape or form.

The support given throughout the four years that I've spent endlessly writing and rewriting this story by the EDSC library team staffed by Ms. Da Silva and Ms. Banister was a major source of inspiration, and of course, their endless hours of divulging literary nit-picks and exchanging personal trash opinions of other, much more successful, books with me also helped. Thank you.

I'd like to thank all of my English teacher from 7th grade right up to where I am now, as without them, this book would only be a rehashed fanfiction that do not deserve to see the light of day.

To the people who've followed me during and after my failed InkShares' crowdfunding campaign for this book, thank you. Without my first group of readers, I believe I wouldn't have found the courage to become a writer. Also, without them, I probably wouldn't have tasted failure so exquisite and bitter as seeing a crowdfunding campaign not garner enough attention and flop. Same could be said to the other authors that I've met and talked with during my first attempt at putting idea-to-paper. Without their suggestions and nit-picks, I also wouldn't have found my writing voice and developed the book to this extent. Special thanks to John Robin, an author who has chosen to take the time to look at work seriously and offer insightful feedback and asked all the questions that needed to be asked in order to shap the development of Peter, Jane, and Albest.

Acknowledging the kind people I've met during the 2014~2018 NaNoWriMo also deserves some mention, as I would likely not have found the time to develop my drafts without this program, and more importantly, the support of this local community of authors and other such talented folks.

To all my friends, you know I would thank you, for being there when I needed it the most, and for being there for me even when I was hurting. But I'm not going name every one of you, because I'm too lazy to do so. Sorry, Khaalid, for never quite being able to spell your name right until the moment it counted. Thanks, Victor, for being the asshole who inspired the character of Albest and then immediately making peace with the fact that he's based on you.

To everyone else that I didn't mention, but I deserved to mention, but forgotten/too last to do so/ decided against/are kidnapped by extra-terrestrial forces to be probed anally: thank you as well. I may not have precisely remembered how you have contributed, but without your help. I probably wouldn't be as decent a guy as I believe I am now.

And lastly, The Readers. Thank you, for making it to the end of this book. Without any readers, an author is just someone wasting their time typing up meaningless words day after day to be read by only themselves.

To Peter, Albest, and Jane, you're not necessarily the best, most well-written, or even the most interesting characters of all time. But you left a mark like a cup of coffee staining my math homework and had subsequently blurred out enough of my working-out to warrant the deduction of half a mark. You mattered. So, hey, so long and thanks for all the fish, enjoy hanging out with a bowl of petunias and a whale, y'all.

Yicheng Liu is an Australian writer and terrible student from Melbourne, Victoria. Made his start as a writer writing shitty AU Fanfictions, arguing over OTPs on fan-forums, and crafting OCs on PbP roleplaying forums, and diversified from there onwards to hone his writing skills. Now in the middle of writing another book. Alive. Likes sushi.